Next to Nature, Art

Books by Penelope Lively

THE ROAD TO LICHFIELD
NOTHING MISSING BUT THE SAMOVAR
TREASURES OF TIME
JUDGEMENT DAY

for children

ASTERCOTE
THE WHISPERING KNIGHTS
THE WILD HUNT OF HAGWORTHY
THE DRIFTWAY
THE GHOST OF THOMAS KEMPE
THE HOUSE IN NORHAM GARDENS
GOING BACK
BOY WITHOUT A NAME
A STITCH IN TIME
FANNY'S SISTER
THE VOYAGE OF QV66
FANNY AND THE MONSTERS
FANNY AND THE BATTLE OF POTTER'S PIECE
THE REVENGE OF SAMUEL STOKES

Next to Nature, Art

Penelope Lively

HEINEMANN : LONDON

William Heinemann Ltd
10 Upper Grosvenor Street, London W1X 9PA
LONDON MELBOURNE TORONTO
JOHANNESBURG AUCKLAND

First published 1982

© Penelope Lively

434 42739 X

Printed and bound in Great Britain by
Biddles Ltd, Guildford and King's Lynn

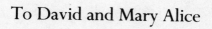

To David and Mary Alice

Chapter One

Landscape with figures. The landscape is the contrived and ordered landscape of around 1740: a terrace dropping down to a prospect which itself is discreetly separated by a ha-ha from the view it contemplates. Trees line the prospect. The view is a wide cup of rural England: bleached fields (for this is mid-summer) and dark drooping trees and criss-crossing hedges, with – if you search carefully – a strategically placed temple in the far distance. But something is wrong. The prospect is a hayfield, the ha-ha smothered in brambles, the terrace shaggy with weeds, the parterre to the side of it blurred almost to invisibility. And, where the eye should be drawn to the cleft in the horizon there is now a road, so that the glint of cars interrupts and distracts. Every half hour or so an aircraft blasts diagonally across, taking off from the American air-base half a mile away.

The figures are a woman and a small boy, upon the terrace, backs to the landscape, facing the house which is the point of it all.

*   *   *

Paula sits on the terrace wall. She is in her late thirties and has tawny hair – much tawny hair – and a remarkable face and long legs. The legs, at this moment, are covered to the ankle by a skirt of material that pretends to be patchwork. Above that she wears a purple T-shirt. She is making a chain of the daisy-like flowers that spring from cracks in the paving and fissures in the wall. From time to time she looks up at the house, a building of elegance and symmetry in perfect accord with its setting, and, like that, in a sad state of decline – the stucco shabby, a disagreeable extension of about 1880 slapped on at one end.

Jason is peeing into the lily-pond. He pees in a wide delicate arc, playing the jet from one lily-pad to another. Jason's hair too is fair and he has the face of a small boy in an advertisement: engaging and healthy and unknowing, the archetypal child. An aircraft crashes past.

"That's a fighter. How do people pee in aeroplanes?"

"They have loos," says Paula. "You'd better pack that in. Here's Toby."

"Why?"

"Because it's bad for the bloody fish, or the frogs or whatever."

"But I wanted to," says Jason.

"Grown-ups," says Paula, "don't do that."

"Why can't grown-ups do what they want?"

Paula yawns. "They can. At least they sort of can. That's just not the kind of thing they want to do."

"What do they want to do?"

"Different things," says Paula crisply. She completes her daisy-chain, hangs it around her neck, and waves to two men who are coming out through the french windows of the house onto the terrace.

Jason also looks towards the men. "Nick came out of Toby's

2

room this morning with just his pants on. He hadn't got any pyjamas."

Paula adjusts her daisy-chain. "Did he now? Well, well. Fancy."

"Is he too poor to have any pyjamas?"

"Frankly, I wouldn't know."

The men arrive, now, at the lily-pond. Toby Standish, owner of Framleigh Hall, and Nick Watson, unemployed graduate of Camberwell School of Art; the one fortyish and slightly balding and the other twenty-two, short, dark and uncertain of manner.

Toby says, "That damn butcher hasn't delivered yet. They're going spare in the kitchen."

"Have you phoned?"

"Yes, Paula, I have phoned. He says his van's on the blink."

"Who's taking the minibus to the station?"

Toby sits down on the wall. "I really have no idea who is taking the blasted minibus to the station." Thin, to the point of concavity, he wears faded jeans and a coloured shirt (he always wears jeans and a coloured shirt), sleeves rolled up and front buttons partly undone, showing his navel and the inward curve of his stomach. He wipes a hand across his forehead, giving an impression of exhaustion held at bay by a fund of nervous energy.

Nick says, to Paula "I think Toby's getting one of his heads. Do you think we should . . ."

"I am not," says Toby, "getting one of my heads. I merely am concerned about providing a meal for sixteen people in three hours' time."

Paula stretches. "Greg will take the minibus to the station and pick up the meat on the way. No problem. I s'pose I'd better check the rooms." She sighs, rises, and wades with sandalled feet through the terrace greenery. She pauses a moment by

3

Nick. "Very choice you are in your stripy cheesecloth today, ducky. Incidentally I could do with a hand in the studio in a minute. I want to move the new piece before the onslaught, and Greg'll be gone to the station. I don't know where the hell Bob is, by the way, he pushed off somewhere this morning."

"Yes, of course, Paula. Would you like me to . . ." But she has already gone, approaching now the open french windows of what was once the drawing room and looking, with her long skirt and piled thick hair, like some vaguely distorted manifestation of the house's past.

There is a silence. Bees, birds, the distant rumble of a combine harvester. "Toby," says Nick. "There's a thing I've been wondering. I've been thinking perhaps . . ."

Toby, now, also rises. "Another time, love, if you don't mind. I've got to see to something." And he too goes away towards the house.

Jason has lain there all the while upon his back. He looks up and sees them through the tangle of daisy and herb robert and periwinkle and rampant bindweed: enormous, like gods walking. They have loud irrelevant voices and legs that go up and up and end in round quacking faces. Paula's face and Toby's face and Nick's face. He makes the sky into a sea, in which people stand on their heads with their feet sticking up. He looks down into this sea and makes fish swim about the heads, goldfish darting through Paula's floating hair, minnows nosing at Toby's forehead.

Framleigh Creative Study Centre, once Framleigh Hall, is nine miles from the market town and railway station towards which Greg, in the Framleigh minibus, is now driving. The village of Framleigh crouches at the gate of the park: pub (the Standish

4

Arms), Mace Superstore, hardware store, greengrocer, school, church, nucleus of old cottages and farmhouses, the whole embraced by a girdle of council housing and bungalows for the retired.

Greg whips through the lanes, driving with one arm on the window ledge. He is a twenty-nine year old poet, American, five years resident in England, eighteen months attached to Framleigh. His brief there is to provide support of various kinds for Paula and inject into the courses that verbal element which has hitherto been lacking and which Toby feels they ought to have. Music, they ought to take in, too; they had a bloke who was doing marvellous things with electronic sound at one point, but he had a flaming row with Paula and went, so that area of expression is neglected at the moment.

For this is nineteen seventy-four, a time when creativity is rated high. And Toby, who shares with his Standish forebears a certain ability to snatch straws from the wind (an eighteenth century Standish curried favour with Fox, and received useful patronage, a nineteenth century one made a packet in the railway boom), has seen the handy combination of his own artistic status and ownership of a large and handsome if run-down ancestral home. Since the environment is also held in high esteem just now he set out initially to bring in that too, Framleigh being surrounded by it, so to speak. But the Framleigh Centre for Field Studies, started at the same time, foundered with the defection of the old school friend and botanist who was meant to be running it but did not, in the end, see eye to eye with Toby over various things. So the Study courses ignore the environment these days (unless you count painting and sculpting it) except for the Nature Trail through the park on which Toby takes course members.

Toby himself is known best as a lithographer and graphic

artist. His allegorical studies, in which figures wander through odd mythical landscapes, and his more abstract swirling prints, called Nature Suites, have been seen in a couple of West End galleries. Quite a few of the people who come on the courses have vaguely heard his name.

This weekend's course is due in ten minutes. Or rather, nine of its members will by then have gathered at the station, getting off various trains from various directions, and will be expecting to be met, as promised in the brochure. The other two are arriving by car and will find the place themselves, coming upon the open but rusty wrought-iron gates opposite the council houses and pausing as they turn in to stare with respect at the park: the avenue of elms (many of them skeletal, victims of the beetle), the plantings of beech and oak, the cows drowsing in the shade. The cows, of course, are not Toby's: they belong to Lamniscaat Farms Ltd., a Dutch company.

Greg stops off to collect the meat, and also a bottle of scotch with which he proposes to sustain himself through the week: the Study Courses are quite tough going for the Framleigh faculty, as Toby likes to call himself, Paula, Greg and Bob. This is a private bottle, for distribution probably only to Paula and conceivably any course member who takes his fancy. Greg then puts his foot down, as time is running short, and arrives in the station yard just as the group outside is coalescing and turning its collective eye, a trifle anxiously, towards the approach road. As the minibus (neatly lettered on one side "Framleigh Creative Study Centre") draws up, they relax.

Six women and three men. The times being what they are, it is not possible to determine occupation, let alone class, by people's dress. The women wear jeans, or long skirts of an Indian cotton in bright colours that, a few years back, would have been regarded as more suitable for bedspreads. They have long hair, for the most part, and look as though they have cultural or artistic connections – work in art galleries, perhaps, or small publishing houses, or in interior decoration. In fact they are a dentist's receptionist, a librarian, two teachers and two married women whose occupation is precisely that. The men are clad as though for a safari or a bout of guerrilla warfare, though this slightly aggressive look is tempered by a good deal of hair around head and face, suggesting aesthetic leanings. They are a university lecturer, a research chemist, and a television camera-man. One of them, and three of the women, are here for emotional reasons, in flight from unsatisfactory personal circumstances by way of spouses, lovers, parents or children.

They are all agreeably impressed by Greg: his silky brown side-burns and his air of ease, his New England voice and his anxious concern for their comfort since in fact this number of people is one too many for the minibus to seat satisfactorily. They pile in, somewhat on top of one another, and ride in a state of interested expectation through the somnolent Warwickshire landscape. A girl called Sue, a librarian from Coventry, sits immediately behind Greg. The sun-tanned back of his neck gives her a slight frisson – he is the one who is a poet, she realizes after a quick peek at the brochure, and she hasn't ever come across a poet before. Keith Harrap, the research chemist, stares out at the fields and trees and villages, composing into pictures that as quickly dissolve, and wishes he'd brought his camera. He lives in Dulwich and doesn't often get into the country. Still, it is to do some painting that he is here; photography hasn't worked out anyway. He has noted the preponderance of women on the course; cursory chat at the station has not revealed them as all that promising, either. The girls are quite attractive, but that seems to be all. Keith looks for rather more than enticing appearance from a woman: he loves his wife, Karen, but feels that she has atrophied of late. Of course that may be his fault (or the children's). And his own creativity is, well, undirected. Evening classes in this and that will no longer do. His potential, he knows, is as yet unrealized; the Framleigh course just might help him to see where he ought to be heading.

They turn into the Framleigh drive a couple of minutes before an old mini driven by a woman called Mary Chambers, who follows them between the elms and into a weedy gravelled circle in front of the house. She sits for a moment in her car as the others disembark, looking at the balustraded steps to the front door, at the top of which stand a man and a woman, who beam in welcome, and a small boy who sits folded with his chin upon his knees and stares.

Toby and Paula, like the gracious host and hostess of a bygone day, stand on the top step and watch the approach of the minibus.

"Just so long as Greg's got that fucking meat," says Toby.

"He will have. Calm down. You'll give yourself a migraine." Paula smooths her billowing skirt, and waves. She wears, around her neck, a chain of wilting daisies.

Toby, too, waves. "And one thing, love, you might mention that I don't care for this amplifier he's playing about with. He was making one hell of a racket yesterday."

"It's part of his film sequence," says Paula. "He's experimenting with sound levels."

"Tell him," snaps Toby.

Paula says with dignity that maybe she'll mention it. She adds, in passing, that Nick never showed up to help her to move the new piece and she thinks she's pulled a muscle in her back.

The course members are now clambering out of the minibus and Toby and Paula descend the steps to greet and welcome.

Two hours later, the visitors have been allocated their rooms, have unpacked their bags and learned their way about the place. They have met Paula, Toby, Greg, Nick and the fifth member of the Framleigh group, Bob, and discovered the studios and the Common Room and the refectory, wandered out onto the terrace and along the prospect and back along the overgrown paths of the old kitchen garden. They have been impressed, bemused or affronted by the place according to age, inclination and experience. None of them remains unmoved, since Framleigh is, in its way, unique.

Designed by William Kent, the house itself is not perhaps outstanding. There are other early eighteenth century country houses of equal or greater grace and elegance. But the park has always been considered a masterpiece, transcended only by Rousham and Stowe, the perfect manifestation of the picturesque: Hogarthian lines of beauty, sham ruins, cascade, grotto, the lot. Twenty-five acres in which the disordered was cunningly turned into a contrivance, in which the physical world was made an artistic product, in which nature became art.

All that, though, was a long time ago, and since then much has happened including the misfortune of several generations of inept Standishes. Toby's father failed to take advantage of either the glad hand of the National Trust or the opportunities offered

9

by mass tourism; Framleigh has gone to seed. What the course members see, as they wander about the place, is a lamentable ruin of what was, overlaid by the tastes of subsequent generations: by Victorian brick, by Edwardian insensitivity and above all by weeds.

During the war the house was taken over by a preparatory school, evacuated from a more hazardous part of the country. The old servants' pantries and the corridor from the kitchen to the dining room are filled to this day with tiers of lockers and a forest of pegs, the faded names stencilled on flaking green paint: J. P. R. Mather, D. Loxton-Smith, Upper 1Vb Games Kit. In the field beyond the ha-ha, where at one end goal-posts stand at a drunken angle, the long grass seems infested yet with the ghostly forms of small boys, purple-kneed on winter afternoons, swarming over one another in the mud.

Elegance is, now, at so many removes as to seem not so much irretrievable as barely to be imagined. In the Common Room – once the drawing room – hangs an oil-painting of the house in its hey-day, spruce and sparkling in a landscape clean as a whistle, the trees and grass manicured, the parterre precise as an architectural diagram. Indeed, there is something diagrammatic about the whole painting, not least the bewigged and beribboned figures parading in the foreground, doll-like men and women impossible to think of as flesh and blood. Thus, too, the house's own previous persona seems fictional, a mythical thing from the pages of a book, its present blurred and muted state far more real and apposite.

In the painting, the houses and park appear as a contrived and ordered island amid the green ocean of the countryside. In contrast, today, the shaggy woodland of Kent's landscaped grounds is an unexpected tumult amongst the disciplined squares and oblongs of agricultural Warwickshire. Many of the trees, of course, have far outgrown the intended scale; elsewhere undergrowth and copses have blunted the original lay-out; the serpentine "rill" has all but vanished in thickets of unquenchable rhododendron. The whole place appears to be held in check only by the estate wall: a disorderly raffish presence alongside the innocent council houses and bungalows displaying their washing, greenhouses and prams where village and the entrance to Framleigh Park meet at the road.

In the same way, the inside of the house has an atmosphere not so much of graceful decay as an insensitivity to change, a kind of deafness and blindness to the world that saddles it now with peeling Edwardian wallpapers, thirties lino shivered into a spiderweb of cracks, wheezing pipes, clanking sanitation and a pervasive smell of damp. Since Toby, when up against it, has sold off most of the remaining paintings and the better pieces of furniture, the rooms are furnished with a combination of Edwardian and thirties stuff, giving way to Habitat in the "visitors'" bedrooms and an element of ethnic cushions, rugs and covers introduced lately by Paula. One of Paula's own pieces, a huge appliqué-work picture of Adam and Eve in brilliant colours hangs above the (original) marble fireplace in the Common Room. The serpent, in puce nylon, coils round the trunk of a corduroy tree from which hang multi-coloured gingham apples. Some more of Paula's work, from her corrugated iron period, is in the hall, occupying the marble niches. Outside, at the apex of the woodland ride and upon the plinth where stood originally the Apollo that Toby's father was obliged to part with at an awkward time in the thirties, is her "Introspective Woman", an abstract sculpture of welded bicycle frames and silver-sprayed nylon fruit netting.

This, then, is the present state of Framleigh, and it is amid this uneasy confusion of social and aesthetic intent that the eleven course members sit down to their first meal, in what was the dining room and is now the refectory. They sit upon long benches at a long table, with Paula, Toby, Greg, Nick and Bob interspersed among them, since togetherness is the ethic of Framleigh. The meal is cooked and dealt out by the two Filipino girls who comprise the Framleigh domestic staff. They are paid subsistence wages bolstered in theory by English lessons given by Paula or Greg when either can find the time or the inclination. The Filipino girls, did they but know it, are perhaps the only element of the place fair and square within the Framleigh tradition. They even sleep in the old servants' garrets.

At the far end of the table, out of earshot of any of the Framleigh contingent, the dentist's receptionist says to Mary Chambers, *sotto voce*, "What I don't quite understand is, are Paula and Toby married? I mean, since you aren't told any surnames."

"The little boy," offers the red-haired teacher opposite, "is hers. There's a resemblance."

"But is he theirs?"

No one can solve this. Mary Chambers, herself mother of three, has been perturbed, earlier, to come upon Jason in the garden hacking at twigs with a penknife of evidently wicked efficiency. No six year old of hers would be let loose with a thing like that. Since criticism is clearly out of place, she confined herself to a demonstration of techniques least likely to end in dismemberment. Down the table, Toby is leaning across to talk beguilingly to Sue, the pretty fair girl from Coventry, who looks

12

gratifyingly beguiled. Paula, in a long dress of what appears to be tapestry, is in earnest discussion with Keith Harrap. Bob, the burly northern potter, is holding forth at the far end, and has his neighbours in stitches. He is a big man, a bear of a man, with muscled arms at which the girls glance and a badger-beard beneath sharp friendly brown eyes. He yarns away, a professional Yorkshireman, and his neighbours beam and giggle, bewitched. Nick is staring at Toby, and looks worried. Greg helps the Filipinos to dish out goulash.

All this watched by Mary Chambers, a quiet woman more given to observation than to participation. She is small, and of no particular colouring, and has one of those faces that somehow fail to lodge in the memory; others can never quite recall who she is. She on the other hand tends to remember people only too well. She is, at the moment, noting the way in which the Framleigh people – Toby and Paula and Greg and Bob; Nick, somehow, does not seem quite to fit in with the others – are different from the course people. They are in some way brighter and louder and more certain. Of course, they are at home and the others are not and are, as yet, on their best behaviour, but even so there appears to be some generic difference. She wonders if it is to do with being artists. Admittedly, some of it is to do with using rather strong language (Paula) and having a rich northern accent (Bob) and being American (Greg) or the owner of a large and old if unkempt house (Toby); but it is also to do with appearing not to care or even be interested in what other people think of you and wearing clothes that are superficially like the clothes everyone else is wearing but also subtly not, and talking to others in a way that is perfectly agreeable and yet somehow makes it clear that there are certain distinctions.

Mary is attending the course at the urging of her husband; she has always done a bit of painting and drawing, and he thinks she should do more. She, on the other hand, is feeling a bit guilty about the expense: they need a new washing-machine, and there is Jane's school trip to France to be thought of. She remembers these things while listening to the conversation around her. The dentist's receptionist continues to discuss their hosts with the red-haired teacher.

"She's very stylish, isn't she? I mean, somehow without trying." They observe, over the goulash, Paula.

"I mean, you'd kind of know, looking at her, that she was somebody interesting. That's true of all of them."

"Bob's ever so nice, isn't he?" says the teacher. "I think I'll do the potting tomorrow."

The dentist's receptionist, who is called Jean Simpson, goes on eyeing Paula while she describes other course centres she has attended. She is an emphatic woman of forty or so and would appear to be something of a connoisseur of such places. She and her husband, she explains, tend to go their own way over hobbies – "But don't get me wrong, everything's fine otherwise" – and she likes a little break on her own from time to time. With an activity of some kind. She tells of a place she went to last year at which you learned to print, on a hand-press. You could print a little book, if you stayed a week. Of course, she says, that wasn't art, really, and the people who ran it weren't artists, exactly, not like here – I mean, they just knew how to do something well. Hertfordshire, it was, and they didn't have the surroundings like they have here, but there were some nice types on the course. "What I like here so far," she goes on, "is the way they're a community. Like a family, only not."

"Families . . ." says the teacher, with a sigh. "Don't give me any of that . . ." She is having husband trouble and hopes, among other things, to find someone nice to talk to during the weekend.

"There's something kind of different about them, here," continues Jean Simpson. "Being here's not like being in the ordinary world."

"Right," agrees the teacher, thinking still and with malevolence of her husband (presently, she hopes, searching the fridge for the supper she has not prepared).

At this point Toby rises to suggest an adjournment to the Common Room for coffee and "a little introduction to Framleigh I like to inflict on people at the beginning of a course". The visitors, obedient and sympathetic, follow him from the refectory.

Toby stands, as he has stood so many times before, beside the marble fireplace and slightly to the right of Adam in Paula's appliqué picture. He allows the audience to settle, clutching its mugs of Nescafé, and runs a hand across his eyes – the quick, nervous gesture typical of his movements. He would much rather, it implies, not be doing this, but since needs must . . .

"Hello, everybody. Well, you've met us all now, and you've seen the place. I just want to give you some idea of what Framleigh's about. The main thing is for you all to feel relaxed while you're here – relaxed and liberated. You're going to work and play and do your own thing and we're here – Paula and I and everyone else – to give you all the help you need and bring you out of yourselves. Paula and I are around the studios all day. There'll be a life-class for anyone who wants it – lino-cutting, etching – potting with Bob in the old barn. Paula's sculpture class in the stables. Afternoons are free for you to do what you like. I take a Nature Trail round the park tomorrow. Wednesday we've got something a bit special laid on. Greg's putting on a poetry workshop for anyone who'd like to drop in. Sunday night by which time we all feel we've known each other a hundred years we usually have a bit of a party. Bring your own bottle. O.K.? Anything you want to know – just nobble one of us."

He pauses and smiles, a warm, inviting smile. "And now, I don't want to be a bore but I'd just like to at this point say a word or two about what I call the Framleigh Ideal." He pauses again, the smile replaced by a responsible, serious look – almost a burdened look. "The thing is, Framleigh's been in my family since it was built and I don't need to tell you it's bloody difficult to keep up a place like this. Vintage cars and lions just wouldn't be my scene, frankly, even if we were in that league. Nor the dead hand of the National Trust; I don't go for museums. Because the point is that I see Framleigh as having a valuable up-to-the-minute today kind of potential as just this: a place where people can get away from ordinary life and find out what's going on inside their own heads. A sort of island – a haven, to be corny – in the ghastly modern world. A place where people can find out about their own creativity and their potential and see where they're going. All of us – you and others who come here and Paula and Greg and Nick and Bob and myself. O.K. – so we're artists and you're not, at least not professional ones. But that's not the point. The point is that we all need somewhere and something like Framleigh – a release, a place where we can really be ourselves, where we can forget about what we've got to do and do what we want to do. Be what we

16

want to be. So that's what I've tried to make Framleigh into. A sanctuary. A creative sanctuary. There! Lecture over! Paula – are you laying on another cup of coffee?"

Later, much later, Framleigh falls quiet. Lights are put out. The Filipino girls, whacked, go straight to sleep. Sue lies in the Habitat bed in Room Five in the visitors' wing and realizes that it is Toby she is in love with and not, as she had at first thought, Greg. Keith Harrap strips his Dulwich semi, in the mind's eye, and re-furnishes it with Paula's appliqué pictures and fun-sculptures. He also strips his wife and re-dresses her in Paula's patchwork skirt and T-shirt worn without bra.

Greg, in the old gun-room that serves now as telephone room, makes two calls to London and one to Boston.

Bob walks back from the village pub in the dark, a trifle unsteadily. Nick reads a thriller in bed and frets.

Jason sleeps. Blamelessly.

Outside, the tawny owl that will feature in Toby's Nature Trail is committing an atrocity upon a field-mouse. Large black slugs come out of cracks in the terrace walls and eat the new young shoots of anything in their path. Further away, Kent's woodland ride is loud with rustlings and screamings. The bulrushes by the stream are full of toads in sexual congress. A cow has a calf in the beech plantation.

Paula, in the largest of the rooms in the wing now reserved to Framleigh faculty, says to Toby "I hear you're having it off with Nick".

"Ah. You do, do you? Little pitchers, I suppose?"

"Little pitchers, as you say."

"I imagine," says Toby thoughtfully, "that we do the most

ghastly things to children." He gets up from the end of the bed, where he has been sitting. "I'm going to have a bath. Incidentally I think we ought to make a rule about no baths for course members after ten."

"You don't love me," says Paula, without emotion.

"No," he agrees. "I did once," he adds, courteously.

Mary Chambers puts out her light and has a conversation in her head with her husband, to whom she tells most things. It is all very free and easy here, she says, Toby who owns it is not at all what you might expect – people say he has a title but doesn't use it, goodness knows if that is true. Then there is Paula who may be his wife though it's not clear – she is rather beautiful and has a way of making you feel inferior though I expect she doesn't mean to. There is an American poet called Greg and a potter called Bob and Nick who finished art school last year. They all seem to have something to do with each other but it is difficult to see exactly what. And there is a little boy called Jason. The house has been lovely once but is rather run down now and the grounds are quite overgrown – it makes you realize what happens when things are not kept under control. Oh, I forgot to tell you the meat for tomorrow night is in the fridge, not the freezer, and Helen should have a clean shirt for school tomorrow. The dinner money is in an envelope on the kitchen shelf.

Chapter Two

Next morning, the course begins in earnest. After breakfast Paula, with an apology for being so boring, mentions a few domestic details. The visitors learn – a little to their surprise, given the cost of the week – that they are expected to make their own beds and, on Wednesday when the Filipino girls get an evening off, do the washing-up. Baths are extra, alas, oil being so astronomical now. They gather, then, upon the terrace where Toby goes round with a clip-board seeing who would like to do what this morning. Standing there in the sunshine, laughing and chatting, the girls in their long bright skirts, they might be a house-party from some other time: Edwardian, or the eighteenth century.

Sue, of course, is going to join Toby's group. Keith Harrap opts for Paula's life class (the life is provided by one of the Filipinos, borrowed from the kitchen for an hour or two and understandably bewildered). Mary Chambers, after some thought, decides also to opt for Toby and a graphic morning. A dark jumpy girl called Tessa is determined to pot with Bob, and lingers anxiously at Toby's elbow as she sees the pottery class filling up. Eventually, they are all distributed and the terrace empties.

The Framleigh workshops are conversions of the old stables and outhouses. Conversion is perhaps a fanciful term, though: adaptation might be better since in many instances legacies of former use remain and are exploited – hayracks have become storage bins for Paula's various raw materials, a mounting-block is a useful stand for a sculpture in progress, pictures hang from the harness hooks in the tack-room. Only the big barn, now the pottery, has been substantially altered within, and this is thanks to Bob's skill at carpentry. The barn is his private empire.

In this respect, though, each of the Framleigh contingent has their own sphere, and there are no encroachments. Toby teaches graphic work and, when he feels inclined, lino-cutting and etching. Paula's range is wide and includes anything she is herself up to at that moment: appliqué-work, a certain amount of straight painting, jewellery, *objets d'art* constructed from plaster of paris and bits of mirror, sculptures made from old tights stuffed with plastic foam fragments and arranged into contorted piles reminiscent sometimes of enormous turds and sometimes of intertwined draught excluders. She is also working out – and sharing her experiences with course members – a new technique involving chicken feathers, plastic flex, dayglo paint and lengths of bicycle chain. When feeling indulgent, she lets them do a bit of batik, or even tie and dye.

Nick helps Toby and sometimes takes a group off on his own into the park for some outdoor work. His real interest is design (he would like to get into textiles eventually) but Toby has a block about that so Nick has not liked to suggest a separate class:

colour, form and line. It is very much in his mind, though, and from time to time when he thinks Toby is feeling receptive, he begins to mention it. So far he has not yet completed the mentioning, because Toby always seems to switch off or go away. Nick does not really know where he is with Toby. Consequently he is obliged to hang around Framleigh practically all the time instead of seriously looking for a job.

Greg's poetry workshop takes many forms. At the moment he is into photography. He has moved on from sound poetry and realizes that not only are words not enough but that ideally word and vision must be fused: the poet *is* the message. Accordingly, where his personal work is concerned, he is experimenting with soft-focus photographs of himself over which will be printed the poems, probably in gothic script. He is also making film recordings of himself verbalizing in a state of free association; the film itself, of course, is the artistic product.

Bob pots, quite simply. It is rumoured that he once worked with Bernard Leach. He is a competent craftsman, as it happens, and would probably be equally good at making chairs, or clocks, or re-fitting an engine or tailoring a suit. He has that meshing of hand and eye, and capacity for taking pains. Not genius, just skill. He has observed, though, that more respect is accorded to art than to craft and has learned to exude a certain mystique: he can teach you to throw an adequate pot, is the implication, but the special something that will lift it into another class – his class – is untransmittable. Nevertheless, the pottery group is by far the most popular, on every course. People like to have a real tangible object to take home. Besides, Bob has an aura: an irresistible mixture of rough Yorkshire machismo and the specialness of his trade. Today, his large clay-covered talented hands rest on Tessa's, his eyes twinkle at her over his beard, his

21

crunchy fisherman's jersey presses up against her back, she feels that strong male artistic vitality. She is shy of him and desperate to please; he is unlike anyone she has ever known. Of course he is different: he is an artist.

There is one other person who should perhaps be mentioned: Jason. Jason is merely there. He does nothing, all day. From an adult point of view, that is.

Thus, this morning, all over Framleigh, people create.

Sue sits in Toby's workshop and scowls in concentration at the easel. She feels – not like herself at all, really. Elated, translated. Like after a drink. It is not so much what she is *doing* – about which she has grave doubts – but being in here at all. With Toby's things on the walls all around: the lithographs and the new suite that is a dream sequence based on *The Waste Land*. "What do you think of it?" Toby had asked and she'd blushed scarlet and said she thought it was super, all those marvellous spirals, the way it sort of led you on . . . And Toby had laid a hand on her arm and said, that's sweet of you, my dear, and now let's see what you can do, why don't we put you here, where the light's good . . . And so here she is, bathed in Framleigh light, her blonde baby-fine hair curtaining her face, her heart running a little fast, drawing. Out of this world.

Mary Chambers is painting the Filipino girl. She notes the problems presented by the texture of the hair, and labours to resolve the difficulty. She is having trouble also with the angle of a knee, and presently tears off the sheet and begins again. Paula's fun-sculpture of a chicken wire and dayglo paint Harlequin keeps catching her eye, and bothers her. She cannot for the life of her find in it anything to admire, and this, too, worries her. Determinedly, she stares at the Filipino girl, who fidgets and yearns for release.

Keith Harrap also paints, though he finds his concentration wandering and thinks the session goes on a bit long for his taste. He decides to try something a bit more material tomorrow: this plaster of paris business maybe, or the fiddling around with wire and flex.

Bob says to Tessa, "How about a jar in the village pub tonight?"

Jason, meanwhile, goes about his own business. He has a friend, Kevin, in tow, who comes up from the village. Kevin is chunky and dark-thatched and looks a miniature version of the burly sensible Warwickshire builder he will one day be. He follows, rather than accompanies, Jason, and falls in with Jason's arrangements. He talks to no one except Jason and observes Framleigh out of the corner of one eye with disbelief and faint mistrust. He is shocked by the absence of a television, suspicious of the food, envious of the fish-ponds and climbable trees, and contemptuous of Toby, Nick, and Greg, who seem to him a right soft lot. He approves of Bob. Paula is so alien, so unlike any other woman he knows, that she might as well be a Martian and he gives her a wide berth. Once, encouraged by Nick and Toby, he got stuck into some paints and produced a wonderfully flamboyant portrait of his family, lined up outside their council house: Mum, Dad, Paul, Sharon and the budgie, all beaming away under a sunny sky in a garden blooming with flowers, washing and a big spotted football. He was embarrassed, though, by the praise that was showered on this effort, which seemed to him neither here nor there, and did not take it home, as was suggested.

Jason and Kevin cross the prospect, leaving a wake of crushed grass. Thigh-high in greenery, dappled with sunlight, dawdling brown-limbed through the sleepy morning, they seem an image of idyllic childhood: a long ago photograph, a scene from the cinema of sensibility, a commercial for Danish bacon. They arrive at the edge of the woodland, and vanish into the undergrowth.

Jason produces three mangled cigarettes from his pocket, and a box of matches. He says, "You can have one too if you want."

Kevin, who has never had a bash at this particular activity, but is not going to let on, eyes him. "Where'd you get 'em?"

"Out of Bob's pocket." Jason lights up, with care, and puffs. "Make yer sick."

"Bob isn't sick. Nor's any of them."

"I done it once," says Kevin casually. "S'not up to much."

Jason, who is inclined to agree, holds the cigarette close to the back of his hand to feel how hot it is. Bored with it, he buries it in a pile of dirt. He strikes matches, one by one, and drops them just in time, as the flame creeps to his fingers.

Kevin, otherwise nurtured, watches in horror and in fascination. "Don't your mum tell you never to do that?"

Jason, who honestly cannot remember Paula's policy on the matter, if any, grunts. He tempts providence a little too far and burns a finger. The grunt turns to a squeak and he sits licking the finger. Kevin's look of anxiety is tinged with smugness. "You shouldn't mess about with them. Matches aren't toys."

24

Jason, examining a pink finger, catches the alien tones of Kevin's mum and scowls. "Balls," he says, in retaliation.

Kevin blinks. Half a mile away, his mum comments once again. Sidestepping the matter, he rolls onto his stomach, shunts himself backwards into the bushes and machine-guns Jason, who drops dead. Overhead, a warbler joins the orchestration of wood-pigeons, tits and a robin. The whole place sings, joyously; shafts of sunlight sift down through the leaves; flowers turn lovely vacant faces to the bees. Jason rises, and dies again. And again.

After lunch (one of the simple country meals promised in the brochure, though the home-baked bread is, Mary Chambers rather suspects, from the nearest supermarket and the local cheese is in fact processed Cheddar) the course members disperse to spend the afternoon according to inclination. Some of the younger ones, setting off in search of the swimming-pool which was also promised, are a touch disappointed to come across it eventually tucked away beyond the kitchen garden and empty but for a deposit of green scum. The pool was in fact installed in the nineteen twenties in response to the requirements of the period, and has been derelict this many a long year. However, they agree, you can't have everything, and, as Sue exclaims: just look at those roses! And, yes, the roses are indeed a sight – Madame Zephirine Drouhon and Etoile d'Hollande and Mermaid, sprawling in uncurbed munificence over the ten foot brick walls that form an L-shaped enclosure to the pool. Sue tucks an Etoile d'Hollande into the cleft of her T-shirt, not knowing quite what she is about, but feeling still a little heady.

Eventually they find the croquet set and play around with

that on the only piece of shaven grass, at the centre of the gravelled sweep in front of the house. It is not quite large enough to be satisfactory.

The Framleigh faculty appear to have vanished, except for Nick who sits uneasily on the terrace, reading and looking up from time to time at the windows.

Mary Chambers goes back to Paula's workshop, to inspect her painting. She finds it unsatisfactory, and takes a sketch block outside. Wandering around, she comes upon the cascade at the start of the woodland ride and decides to have a go at that. The cascade no longer cascades, but is green and mossy and of tricky texture. She settles happily for the next couple of hours.

Toby, in fact, is in his room with migraine, a not uncommon event on the opening day of a course. Nick, presently, comes up and stands uncertainly at the foot of the bed. "Should I tell that girl to stop hoovering, Toby?"

"No, don't bother. You can turn the blasted collared doves off if you like. Monotonous bloody racket."

"Collared doves?"

"Birds, to you. Never mind."

"I wish I could do something."

"Not to worry. It'll go. Things do."

Nick hovers. "Shall I just leave you alone for a bit?"

"You do that."

Paula and Greg are working together on a recording session in the disused billiard room. Greg sits on a kitchen chair against a background of draped hessian. His right leg is over his left knee and he stares rigidly and expressionlessly at the camera, wielded by Paula.

"O.K." says Paula, "I'm ready if you are. Shall we go?"

Greg nods.

There is silence, except for the whirr of the camera. One minute, a minute and a half. Paula shuts off the camera and says, "I thought we were going to start?"

"I did start," says Greg. "That's part of it."

"Oh *Christ! Sorry.* I'll start again."

The camera whirrs once more. Two minutes. Greg uncrosses his legs and puts the left over the right. He says "Shit".

Paula looks up, a trifle peeved. "What?"

"O.K." says Greg wearily. "Cut again."

Paula puts her hand to her forehead. "Christ, *sorry* Greg. I didn't realize you'd begun. God, I'm just not with it today."

She resumes filming. The opening sequence, this time, is prolonged to two and a half minutes. Then Greg says "Shit". He stares blankly at the camera. After a further fifteen seconds he continues, conversationally, "He was a shit, you know". This is followed by a sequence of rapid speech during which Greg leans forward to address the camera more intimately. "I'm telling you, my father was a shit. Like, there was no way we could ever talk to each other. We were in a conflict situation right from the start. O.K. – so it's a standard set-up but what I'm trying to figure out is . . ." He continues along these lines for eight minutes, before attempting to draw some conclusions. ". . . I was like messed up through and through by the time I was fifteen, right? A piece of human wreckage, that's me. So the next ten years I try to work it out one way or another, get myself straight, find out who I am. I go through college and all that time my life's so much crap. I don't see how there's any way I can get myself out of it. And then I start writing and it begins to come together. At last I'm getting it together. I realize that art is cathartic, it's got to be . . ." There is a pause, during which Greg may or may not be thinking, after which he continues for another five minutes and comes to an abrupt stop. Paula raises her eyebrows in query. Greg nods and she shuts the camera off. Greg rises and stretches.

"That was fantastic, Greg. It went really well today."

"I'm reckoning on having the text printed, of course."

"Of course. The bit about your early work was marvellous. Actually it was just how I felt when I first got into sculpture, that wonderful feeling that now at last one was . . ."

"Right," says Greg. "What about the final section?"

"It was great. It's the directness that's so marvellous. And the way you sort of don't quite say things."

"It's what I'm all about," says Greg simply.

In the late afternoon course and faculty are re-united for another spell of studio work before dinner. Toby's migraine has persisted so Nick supervises his group. Sue, who has waited in a ferment to see Toby's stooped figure come in at the door, feels her stomach plummet in disappointment: another two hours is too long to go . . . Nick looks at Mary Chambers' sketch of the cascade and sees to his surprise that it is good; he tells her so, nervously, not knowing if this will be all right with Toby, and Mary is equally surprised.

There is much chatter and banter at supper. Everyone knows everyone else by now; alliances have been formed; hair is let down. Toby does not appear but it is said that he will be coming later. There is a tension between Keith and a rather garrulous elderly doctor both of whom dive for the vacant place beside Paula, but Paula herself deftly sorts this out by shifting further down the table so that both can be accommodated. Keith wants to have a quiet talk to her about life in general and the ways in which he feels he is not properly fulfilling himself; the doctor wants to hold forth about Art. Paula, in the event, keeps both of them quiet by talking at length of her work and where it has come from and where it is going and the hang-ups that have prevented it getting further. She is wearing a great deal of cream-coloured cheesecloth and her long thick hair is kept back with a flowered cotton scarf. She talks and talks and Keith silently compares this world with his own, in which the women of the profession dart around in white overalls and are crisply efficient with formulae and figures. He becomes even more convinced that he may have made the most ghastly mistake, way back.

Greg sits at one end of the table and is terribly nice to everyone. He remembers all their names and uses them frequently. In fact he contrives to make each one feel that they are the person he most wanted to talk to; he speaks of the problems of his profession and the literary scene both sides of the Atlantic and his place within or rather without it and impresses all with his fluency and wit.

Nick is opposite Mary Chambers. He is worrying about Toby and how Toby feels, or, he fears, doesn't feel about him and at first can think of nothing to say. But she asks him about his work and presently he is talking about how he would like to go into design and the funny thing is she has some really rather sensible things to say, suggestions to make; she doesn't seem, on the face of it, that kind of person. She wonders if he gets much chance to work here, at Framleigh, and Nick finds himself explaining how he is always meaning to ask Toby . . . but somehow . . . and of course Toby needs him to do other things. She listens, and the large not very expressive eyes watch; they have a way, Nick thinks, of watching beyond what has actually been said, as though they saw round corners. He emphasizes how awfully kind Toby has been, really; that seems necessary. She nods.

After supper there is Nescafé in the Common Room and then Greg gives a poetry reading. He reads some Ginsberg to start with but soon drops that for his own stuff. The course members listen with attention, realizing that they are being offered a rather special experience; some of the poems, as Greg explains, are still in draft form so there is an opportunity to observe the creative process at work. He reads six drafts of one, minutely different. Some of the audience cannot quite follow it.

Mary Chambers follows Greg's poems, up to a point. They are all about Greg. This is interesting, but also only up to a point. Mary doesn't want to be nasty, but she hasn't actually so far found Greg all that interesting. Pleasant enough, but in a way a bit ordinary, though she supposes that as a poet he can't really be. And also she has a feeling that poetry ought to make you look at things differently, whether it be feelings or the world or an idea or whatever. It should open things up. Greg's, insofar as it is that straightforward, is clamped inside his own head.

Keith Harrap has the odd doubt, also. But he can see from Paula's rapt expression that she admires, so he doubts his own doubts, which is unsettling.

Toby slips into the room at some point, unnoticed until gradually people realize he is there, sitting arms folded on a window-seat. Sue goes hot and cold all over.

Bob is not present. Neither is the dark jumpy girl, Tessa.

The reading, eventually, ends. Paula says she has some sorting out to do in the kitchen and goes off, having warmly wished everyone goodnight and hoped that they feel Framleigh up to expectations. There are suitably warm murmurings in response. Toby also leaves, followed after a few minutes by Nick, and so presently does Greg, after giving instructions about switching off lights and shutting doors.

Those course members who are left sit on for a while, chatting. The chat, for the most part, focuses on Framleigh. Jean Simpson reiterates her admiration of the family feel that there is here. Others, more sceptical of the pleasures of family life, extol the apartness of it all, the sense of being somewhere special, the detachment from the real world. I mean, someone says, outside, in real life, you feel everything's a muddle, everyone's out for what they can get, it's me all the way. Here, they've got a sort of perspective, know what I mean? There's things beyond just people that are important. Right?

Words like order and synthesis and integrity are handed around. And alienation, the times being as they are. It is agreed that the Framleigh people are into all or most of these, depending on the value accorded to whichever concept by whoever is speaking.

The chat becomes more desultory. They go to bed.

Sue lies in the Habitat bed in Room Five on the first floor corridor and thinks of Toby. She wonders where Toby sleeps. At the top of the small flight of stairs by the refectory is a door marked PRIVATE; through this door she has seen pass, at different times, Toby, Paula, Jason, Nick and Greg. In her head, now, she passes through this door herself, ectoplasmic, indifferent to the resistance of wood and fact, and then through another. She stands at the foot of a bed in which Toby lies wearing – no, not wearing pyjamas – reading . . . reading poetry. Not, as it happens, Greg's poetry.

He looks up. "I thought you'd come," he says. He pulls back the sheet, his eyes on her face. "Get your things off. I've been waiting." Slowly, she peels the jeans down over her thighs.

Tessa, stumbling with Bob through the darkened park, steps in a cow-pat and is too chagrined to mention the matter.

Toby, a furled copy of *The Times* under his arm, looks in on Paula to complain about a dripping tap in the bathroom. Paula, sitting up in bed filing her nails, peevishly returns the blame. She adds that those girls in the kitchen are being bloody-minded, they want more money. "They can't have more money," says Toby. "It simply isn't on. There isn't any, apart from anything else."

Paula replies that in that case he can tell them himself. Toby pads away to his own room where he gets into bed, switches on the bedside light and turns to the property page of *The Times*.

Chapter Three

Jason, at six-thirty in the morning, wakes, blinks, and arises into instant activity. He trampolines upon the bed, then, bored with this, picks slivers of paint from the battered woodwork of the window-frame. He sees, outside, trees waist-deep in mist, sunshine in swirling shafts. Flights of birds.

He patters across the corridor to Paula's room. He quietly turns the handle and peeks round the door. Paula and Greg are in the bed having what he supposes to be some kind of fight, which seems a bit funny since he thought they were best friends. Paula said they were, once. But the heaving bedclothes do not that much interest him and he goes away.

He returns to his room and gets dressed. Down in the kitchen he ignores the blandishments of the Filipino girls, who are fond of children, and helps himself to cold macaroni cheese from the larder, and hunks of bread and peanut butter.

He goes out, into the mist that is melting now under the streaming sunshine. He wades through the long wet grass of the prospect and takes a private path through the trees and into the kitchen garden, where he wanders down the grassy alley beside the old herbaceous border, a battlefield these days where huge clumps of white daisies and goldenrod loudly triumph. At the far end of the alley he sees one of the people on the course, one of the ladies, the nice one who showed him how to make arrows with his penknife. She is on her hands and knees with her face almost on the grass, quite still, which interests him mildly. He wonders if she has a pain in her tummy, or if she has lost something, or what. At this moment he remembers suddenly his fly-trap in the old dovecote, and forgets her at once.

There are two flies in the fly-trap, fizzing. Jason takes one out between finger and thumb and stares at it. After a moment he gingerly pulls off its wings and observes the gyrations of what remains. After a minute, though, he wishes he had not done this; it gives him a funny feeling inside and he leaves the dovecote in a hurry.

Mary Chambers, waking early, has gone out for a stroll before breakfast. She walks along the herbaceous border, thinking what a pity it has been so neglected. There has been rain in the night which has beaten down a clump of aquilegias: pale gold trumpets are scattered all over the grass. And among these fallen blooms, she sees, are two very large black slugs. She stoops to look more closely and sees that the slugs are grazing on the aquilegia trumpets, grazing just like sheep. There is an atmosphere of unhurried contentment down there on the rain-sodden grass. The slugs are black and shiny, with a smooth mantle behind the head giving way to a complex pleated area, like taffeta or watered silk. And there they are, chomping away: Mary, down now with her head a few inches above them, realizes that she can actually hear them grazing, small delicate tearing sounds. The larger of the two eats deliberately and in a considered way, contemplating the aquilegia blossom and then opening a mouth that is lined with pink. Teeth? She takes her glasses off (for the very myopic, that is the only solution) but still cannot quite see.

The aquilegia, she knows, is *aquilegia longissima*, a particularly pretty one. She wishes she knew the name of the slugs, so very far removed from the kind of thing you find in a lettuce, or lurking beneath flower-pots. The elephants of the slug world: impressive in their way.

Bob, too, is up early. Last night didn't work out according to plan; he'd thought he had her nicely warmed up but the girl scarpered as soon as they got in, in a tizz about something or other.

He sets up the studio for the morning's work. At the far end, concealed by a hessian curtain from the gaze of course members, is a stack of fired pots awaiting collection by the Birmingham department store which has ordered them: three dozen toby jugs in a viscous yellow glaze. The toby jugs are a new departure, less tricky than the garden gnomes which preceded them; the Birmingham buyer is very taken and talking of an additional line in thatched-cottage honeypots. He says Bob's work has individuality, it's out of the common run. Bob checks the toby jugs for flaws and re-draws the curtain, whistling.

Framleigh, in many ways, is a piece of cake. He reckons on another year or two at least, given a few things which need working out. Very adequate facilities, a regular supply of crumpet, a reasonable cash flow. An improvement on the

Somerset village where, for two years previously, Bob struggled to keep a pottery going. The trouble there was that every other Somerset village within a radius of twenty miles also had a resident potter; the market, even in the crowded summer months, simply could not sustain the competition. You could end up giving the stuff away. Curiously, he'd found that the higher you shoved the prices and the more sparsely you displayed the pots the more of them you shifted. People seemed to reckon that if they'd paid through the nose for something it must be good, certain kind of people at any rate. Not that the things weren't good, bloody good come to that, he was too fastidious a craftsmen to tolerate a dud. The toby jugs, in their way, are masterpieces. And he could see the point of preferring to be surrounded by decently made objects; most of the junk Toby and Paula have at Framleigh turns him up, frankly. But it went beyond that, with some people: it was as though by the possession of a chunk of art, so-called, they acquired its mystique, as well. It was this observation that had decided Bob to get out of the craft circuit and move further into art proper. He ran into Toby at a party in London, got talking, paid a visit to Framleigh, and the two of them recognized a possibility of mutual convenience.

He checks the benches and the wheels to make sure that all is ready for the morning's work: a tidy-minded, methodical man. And goes back to the house to collect his group.

It is another lovely day. The party gathers again on the terrace in the sunshine; Toby patrols once more with his clip-board. This morning, though, everyone is more relaxed; they know where they are now, at Framleigh.

*   *   *

36

"This afternoon," says Toby, "I do the Nature Trail, for anyone who fancies a spot of nature."

"And I should jolly well hope you do," Paula breaks in. "Toby's fantastically knowledgeable about the birds and the bees."

Toby lays a tolerant but quietening hand on her arm. "That's straight after lunch, and this morning we split up as yesterday. Now, let's see . . . Sue, would you like a go in the pottery studio?"

And Sue, who does not know how to counter this suggestion, sees her world collapse, at least until lunch-time.

Keith Harrap, more adept, is able to attach himself once more to Paula's group.

Mary Chambers, a little to Toby's surprise, says that she thinks she will go to Greg's poetry workshop. For a moment Toby, who seldom notices other people, is visited by doubts; he wonders if this suburban housewife is really going to care much for Greg's kind of thing.

Everyone accommodated, the terrace empties. Only Jason remains, curled up in the cracked and pedestal-less bowl of an urn. He is, in fact, at sea on a life-raft, rocked by the waves, protected by enormous whales, in communion with the gulls.

"Art," says Greg, "being creative, being able to get it together, is just a question of whether you've got it or not. Being a writer, being really into words, projecting, is either what you're about, or it isn't. If it isn't, then there's no way you're going to be."

"Easy with that clay, love," says Bob. "Gently does it. Stroke it like you were stroking your boyfriend, eh?" And Jean Simpson, many years married, flushes and giggles.

*　　　*　　　*

37

"Today, children," says Paula, "I think we'll try some plaster-work. Something nice and tactile." And she beams upon them, a munificent earth-mother – elemental, wise – handing out goodies by way of plaster of paris and innumerable coloured beads.

Toby, leaving his group for a while in Nick's care, slumps in the leather armchair in the gun-room, one leg hooked over the arm. He holds the telephone receiver to his ear and listens to the voice that crackles from it.

"One million five," says the man in London. "That's a lot of money, Mr Standish."

"Framleigh," says Toby, "is unique." He picks a strand of horsehair from a slit in the leather and winds it round his finger.

"The surveyor's preliminary report has suggested to the Bank a figure of something like a hundred thousand to put the place in some kind of order."

Toby raises his eyes to the ceiling, the paint of which is kippered a reddish brown by years of open fires. He shrugs. He says, in silken tones, "It depends, of course, to what extent you're going to, um, adjust the character of the place. You realize you're dealing with a Grade 1 listed building? Leading architectural experts consider that Framleigh . . . "

"The nature of any renovations," says the man in London crisply, "will naturally be the concern of the purchaser."

"Oh, absolutely. I was merely stressing what one might call the heritage side of things. Not of course quantifiable in any cash sense, which is what makes it so difficult to arrive at figures in this kind of negotiation."

"The figure we're talking of," says the man in London, "if we talk at all, is seven hundred and fifty thousand. If we talk at all."

"Ah," says Toby softly. He seems to ponder for a moment. "And then of course there is the question of the Bank's financial support of the Framleigh Creative Centre once the conversion and enlargement of the stable block is completed and we move over there."

"That side of the arrangement, frankly, Mr Standish, is the one that is meeting with least enthusiasm from other members of my Board."

"What I envisage," continues Toby, "is a scheme whereby you people share in some of the prestige of the Centre."

"And pick up the bills?" enquires the man in London.

There is a pause. Toby stares through the red and blue stained glass porthole window of the gun-room (nineteen thirty-two and conceivably, it occurs to him at this moment, a saleable or shortly-to-be-saleable commodity – this stuff is beginning to arouse interest). "The Framleigh Foundation is what I have in mind. Something along those lines. With your organization's name very prominent in the literature. A fascinating, um, interdependence of commerce and art."

"Interdependence is an interesting word," says the man in London, "under the circumstances. Like show-jumping, do you mean? Take your fences by courtesy of Imperial Tobacco."

"Art . . ." begins Toby.

"Oh, quite," says the man in London. "Look, Mr Standish, I have a meeting in two minutes from now. We'll come back to you on this, if we may. As I say, there's a great deal that my Board isn't happy about. Our Chairman, Sir Henry Butters, may be in your part of the world this weekend in which case he thought he might run over to Framleigh and have a look round, if that's all right with you. Good to hear from you, Mr Standish."

Toby puts the receiver down. He unfurls himself from the

armchair and goes out into the hall. There, he meets Paula, just coming in from her session in the studio. She says, "Oh – were you phoning that blasted plumber? He still hasn't come."

"No, the heating people. By the way, next time you're in Woodbury go into the antique place and ask them if they're interested in thirties stained glass yet."

And the sun benignly shines. When the members of the course emerge, at lunch-time, it is high and hot and when, a couple of hours later, those who wish to be taken on Toby's Nature Trail gather on the terrace it is hanging leaden in the dead centre of the prospect, smiting the landscape with lethargy.

"All here?" says Toby. "Right, then, let's get going," and the group, wedge-shaped, Toby at its head, straggles off down the steps and across the grass in the direction of the woodland way. At the last minute Nick comes hurrying from the house calling, "O.K. if I come too, Toby? I haven't actually ever done the Trail". And Toby waves, laconic, a downward motioning of the hand that seems to say: feel free, suit yourself, who cares.

Among the trees, there is downy sunlight and the continuous comforting rhythm of wood-pigeons. Pale woodland flowers push up through the leaf-mould; plump cushions of emerald moss cling to trunks and branches. Toby talks of oaks, sessile and pedunculate, of hard and soft wood, of squirrel damage. He points out ecological balances; he shows how the world is less random than you might think.

"There is a parallel there, of course," says the elderly doctor earnestly, "with art. The imposition of the rational upon the irrational, the creation of order out of disorder."

Toby, haloed by a shaft of sunlight, smiles. "That, if I may say so, is very much a non-artist's response. One isn't really concerned with making nice patterns. Art is essentially expressive."

The doctor, discomfited, retires to the back of the group.

Toby leads them to a clearing and waves them into silence. "Ssh! You should be able to hear about five different kinds of birdsong from here."

They stand, straining their ears, sorting sounds. Nick, at Toby's elbow, stares down at dead leaves and feels miserable. Sue, furtively, gazes at Toby. The doctor studies a fungus and rather wishes he had not come. Mary Chambers recognizes a chaffinch and a blue tit. Keith Harrap feels like a tourist in Westminster Abbey.

"Nuthatch," says Toby. "That's a bit of luck for you." The group murmurs in gratitude.

They emerge into the more open atmosphere of Kent's woodland ride and proceed towards the central point, the intersection of three such paths. From time to time they pause for Toby to indicate areas of interest: a patch of wild garlic, the tracks of a fallow deer, a dead tree-trunk acting as host to three different mosses and clumps of saffron mushrooms. "Isn't this wood-sorrel?" asks Tessa and Toby lays a hand across her shoulders saying, "Clever girl, go to the top of the class". The sight of his hand on Tessa's flesh occasions for both Sue and Nick a sick folding of the stomach.

The doctor, determined to recover lost face, lectures Keith on theories of the picturesque. "It's the cult of the irregular, you see. And the natural. But the point is that the whole thing has to make a picture. You compose nature into a picture. Interesting idea, I've always thought."

"Mmn," says Keith.

Above them, a robin pours out song of amazing complexity. "Doesn't he sound happy?" says Tessa.

The doctor, his self-esteem restored, chuckles. "That, my dear, is the pathetic fallacy at work."

Tessa stares. "Come again?"

"Frankly," says Toby, "it's sex, neither more nor less. I think we'll turn off down here. Mind yourselves on that wire."

Tessa stiffens with embarrassment. Is he getting at her? Does he know about . . .? In any case that word always makes her feel funny. She is a stocky girl with a high colour and a black fringe almost to her eyebrows: not pretty but tantalizing to men, a fact she has not yet realized.

They are on one of the serpentine paths now, winding up a slope towards the grotto. The undergrowth is dense here, the path itself almost impenetrable at points. "Go ahead, Nick, will you," says Toby. "Slash at those brambles a bit."

From behind someone calls out, "What's that awful smell?"

Toby halts. There is, indeed, a stench of putrefaction, towards the source of which they seem to be heading.

"It's something dead," pronounces the doctor.

Nick pales, he looks queasy. "Actually, Toby, it's silly I know but I've got a sort of phobia about dead things. D'you mind if I . . ."

Toby contemplates him; he looks beyond him down the path and faintly smiles. Behind, the group hovers. "Don't be ridiculous. It'll be a fox, I imagine. We'll have to bury it. Probably a bit further along the path. Go on."

"Please, Toby . . ."

"Go *on*," says Toby, "you're holding us all up."

"Look, I'll go in front," offers Keith. "I've got a cast-iron stomach." But Nick is already stumbling ahead. Once he puts a hand to his mouth and retches.

The smell is appalling. There is also, now, the buzzing of a mass of flies. "Ugh," says Tessa. "I don't like this."

Nick rounds a bend in the path, hesitates, gives a kind of squawk and turns heaving into the bushes. On the far side, in a clearing, huge clouds of black flies fume up from the leaf-mould.

Keith begins to laugh. "It's a bloody mushroom!"

Three or four phallic knobs, coated with insects, stick up from the ground. Toby takes a branch and hits one of them. It disintegrates, releasing more vile smell and a gust of flies. Nick, green, watches from ten yards off.

"My dear Nick," says Toby. "You shouldn't be so absurdly squeamish. Nature's like that. Didn't you know?" He destroys the rest of the stinkhorns. "Interesting species, actually. It's not quite clear how they fit into the scheme of things, though. If you're through with the display of sensitivity, Nick, would you mind leading on?"

And the birds sing. And the flowers nod their seraphic faces to the bees and the butterflies.

The path winds on to emerge at last into an open grassy space dominated at one end by Kent's grotto. The grotto itself commands a view down a slope and out over open countryside through a clearing in the trees. There, time was, you culminated your stroll with a break for contemplation. The spring around which the grotto was built has ceased to erupt elegantly from a niche within and now dribbles out all over the place, so that much of the floor is sodden. The basin beneath the niche is empty except for wet leaves.

"Impressive," says the doctor. "All right if we have a look round?"

Toby sits down on the grass beyond the grotto. "Go ahead. We'll take a break for a few minutes anyway."

The group disperses. Mary Chambers examines a tangle of flowers and tries to put names to things. Sue and Nick place themselves on opposite sides of Toby at a couple of yards distance and sit in electric silence, unaware of each other.

Toby draws attention to the distant call of an owl.

"Goodness . . ." says Sue, "I thought they only came out at night."

"Not at all," says Toby. "Tawnies are quite often about by day. Another misconception." He turns on Sue his deprecating, charming smile. "Nothing in this world is ever as one thinks, haven't you learned that yet, Sue?"

Nick, with the face of a punished child, pulls clover heads to pieces.

The doctor, accompanied by one or two others, inspects the grotto. They pick their way gingerly around the mud on the floor, touch the encrustations of shells, speculate about the other niche in which once stood the marble statue of Aphrodite – also disposed of by Toby's father during a period of financial embarrassment. They observe the old mattress standing on its end in the drier area, and think its presence a pity. They emerge and comment to one another upon the growths of ferns around and above the grotto. The doctor claims to be something of an authority on ferns; that clump right on the top, he says, is a rather unusual species. Slightly to the alarm of his younger companions, he begins awkwardly to scramble up the stony slippery side of the grotto, to take a closer look. Here, says one of the younger men, let me . . . Careful on that wet stone . . . But the doctor declares himself perfectly safe – did a lot of rock-climbing at one time in fact, there we are, I can reach it now . . .

The fall, in fact, is only a matter of four or five feet, and onto soft ground at that. He comes down sideways with a thump that makes every one look over to the grotto, the immediate response one of embarrassment rather than concern. They expect to see an elderly man humiliated. It is only two or three people who see that his head, jerking back as he falls, has struck the projecting edge of a rock.

These, hurrying towards him rather faster than the rest, see that humiliation does not enter into it, the doctor being unconscious.

"Oh look!" cries Tessa, her hand to her mouth, "he's bleeding like mad!"

Nick, who has come forward with the others, turns hastily away.

The doctor, head to one side, mouth slightly open, lies sprawled upon the grass. The blood, in fact, is not copious but creeps in separate trickles down the side of the scalp, seeping into the ground. A fly arrives and settles. No one, for several seconds, does anything but stare. Then, as though by common consent, they all turn to Toby.

Toby's expression – for anyone who knows him well – is one of furious irritation. The group, lacking such familiarity, take it for concern, and wait for guidance.

Illness repels him: old men coughing on park benches, hunched whimpering children, the messy ailments of women. Unmoved himself by sympathy, he has none for others. "It might be you," Paula shouted at him once from a hospital bed, having something whipped out or put in; Toby, knowing it would not, touched her hand and loped away down the ward. "We all come to it," his father mumbled, disgusting in a wheelchair, egg on his stubbly chin; Toby stared at him in incomprehension.

He says, "What a damn stupid thing to happen."

The group rustles, not quite happy at this. Mary Chambers gets down on her knees beside the doctor. Someone says "I don't think we should move him."

45

"Do you," Keith Harrap asks Toby," know anything about first aid?"

"Not a blind thing."

Someone else murmurs about the kiss of life.

"I don't think so," says Mary Chambers. "Not for this. He's breathing, after all. It may only be superficial. Head injuries always do bleed a lot, I believe."

Toby wipes a hand across his forehead. "Christ. That's all one needed. These courses are enough of a strain without anything idiotic like this."

The group, disturbed, rustles again.

"I think," says Keith, "we'll have to get an ambulance." He looks at Toby "Don't you think so?"

"Oh, *Christ* . . ." snaps Toby.

Someone observes that it is going to be awfully awkward being so far from the road.

Toby raises exasperated eyebrows, sighs. "I cannot, I absolutely cannot, have some bloody great vehicle driven down the woodland way."

Mary Chambers stands up. "I do honestly think we ought to do something rather quickly."

"Should I go to the house and phone?" suggests Keith.

Toby, wiping his forehead again, appears to nod.

"Or would it be better perhaps if you did?"

"The nearest hospital's at Woodbury," says Toby, "renowned for inefficiency, I believe. I shouldn't care to fetch up there myself."

Mary Chambers, on her knees once more, mopping the doctor's head with a tissue, looks up. "There presumably isn't any choice. I think Toby should go since he knows the number and so forth and can tell them the nearest point to bring the ambulance to. And anyone else who'd rather. I'll stay here and maybe you would, Keith, and someone else, just in case."

Toby, sighing again, makes a gesture of acquiescence. He sets off, at a pace that suggests weariness rather than urgency, followed by a straggling file of those members of the group who have decided that their continued presence is of no help.

Mary Chambers, Keith Harrap and Tessa, left in the tranquillity of the clearing, stand awkwardly around the prone figure of the doctor. A further attempt is made to mop up the blood with tissues. Keith points out the heavy breathing, and hopes it is a good sign. Nick, forgotten and unnoticed, hovers in isolation some distance away. Belts of light drive across the trees, creating a myriad shades of green. A small brown butterfly settles on the doctor's trousers, opening and closing its wings to the sun.

And Mary, much later, telephones her husband. A man, she says, fell off the top of a grotto and hurt his head but apparently it is only concussion, there will be no long-term damage. Grotto? says her husband, doubtfully. But Mary is talking now of some business with a Nature Trail and a mushroom and someone who knew something all along. Human nature, enquires her husband, or the other kind? There was rather a lot of both today, replies Mary. Well, says her husband, so long as it's worth it to which Mary answers a trifle sharply, he feels, that she can't know that yet, can she? We couldn't, he says, find Helen's gym things and I'm afraid the cat was sick in the hall last night. Mary, in the Framleigh gun-room, stares at a heap of stringless airy tennis rackets; the gym things, she snaps, are in a bag under her bed, as she should know, and the cat must be put in the downstairs loo when you go to bed.

Chapter Four

"No way," they can hear Paula shouting, "do I do the damn cooking. Let's get that straight, right?"

Doors, throughout Framleigh, tend to stand open. From the Common Room you can hear the clatter of dishes in the kitchen and refectory. And voices. This morning, Wednesday morning, there are no dishes, only voices. Paula's, loud, and Toby's and Greg's and Nick's, less loud. In the Common Room, the course members, risen and descended but as yet unbreakfasted, fall silent and listen. It is not difficult to pick up what has happened. The Filipino girls, overnight, have packed their bags and left. In a kitchen laden with unwashed crockery the Framleigh faculty are assessing the situation. Paula's voice rises and falls. Toby is heard to say that she should never have bloody well taken them on in the first place, Dutch girls have always worked out better. Greg suggests that everybody cool it. Nick twitters. There is a crash and sound of breakage, as though the discussion is moving onto another plane. Paula is asking what Toby has to suggest

48

and Toby responds with icy and not quite audible politeness and Greg says look, let's quit that stuff, you two . . . And Jason can be heard loudly and imperviously demanding something to eat.

Sue says, with a nervous giggle, "It doesn't sound as if we're going to get any breakfast, does it?"

"Of course," observes the dentist's receptionist, "you can't really expect people like them to be terribly practical, can you, when it comes to a crisis? I mean, with their temperaments."

Keith stares out of the french windows, disconcerted; he has caught in Paula's voice a tone eerily similar to the peevishness of his mother's domestic row language. His mother, of whom he is fond but unadmiring, is a vet's wife active in the Townswomen's Guild. There must be some mistake.

He says "I think we'd better offer to lend a hand."

"In point of fact," says Toby, "it's made me wonder if we shouldn't re-think the entire staffing situation." He looks thoughtfully at Greg and Paula. "Switch over to a commune arrangement of some kind."

Greg points out that if you make it a regular thing for the course members to do the cooking and wash the dishes, and it isn't a bad idea, you'd maybe have to lower the fees.

Toby thinks not necessarily. He is wondering if you couldn't introduce a sideline by way of Creative Cookery, that sort of thing . . .

"I don't mind having a go at that," says Paula. "It might be amusing."

There will always, Greg considers, be the awkward cuss who thinks he is being exploited.

"Nonsense," declares Paula. "They like it. Look at this lot – they're only too pleased to set to and get things sorted out. Rotas for this and that and Christ knows what. People like them can cope with that sort of thing. It's what they're for, basically."

"You're an elitist, Paula" says Toby.

"If that's meant to be rude I don't bloody well care at the moment."

"It was a statement, merely."

"Pushing it a little," says Greg, "for a guy born into a place like this."

"Right!"

Toby says coldly, "I thought we were discussing the future staffing set-up, but apparently not. In which case I'm going to have a rest. I'd prefer not to be disturbed." He goes.

After a moment Paula says, "Toby's so incredibly self-centred it just isn't true."

"Right," agrees Greg. He lays a soothing hand on her thigh, which Paula almost immediately covers with her own.

"I might come back to America with you next year."

Greg, under the pretext of scratching his wrist, withdraws his hand. He is not planning to return to America just yet. The Fellowship in Creative Writing at a small mid-west university to which he frequently refers has not in fact been offered. He is planning, since there is nothing better around for the moment, to stay at Framleigh until something turns up. One or two straws are in the wind, but none, as yet, secured.

"You know, Paula, you could be getting Toby wrong. O.K. – so he's selfish but I'm sure he has a very genuine love for you."

Paula turns to look at him with an expression of undisguised astonishment.

"You're a part of Framleigh," Greg goes on, with a sigh.

"I can't be responsible for destroying a very real and creative relationship. I mean you and Framleigh as well as you and Toby."

"It sounds as though I'm a bit of furniture," says Paula with dissatisfaction.

"Toby has a deeply recessive personality. He's into self-consideration but he's still a very worthwhile person. He needs you."

Paula gives him another look of surprise; what he says is disconcerting not so much because of content (though that is, too) but because she has never before heard him give this kind of reflective attention to anyone other than himself. She says "Yes, well . . . We'll see."

Greg pats her thigh again. "Attagirl."

Kevin sidles into the Framleigh kitchen, in which people bustle. There are rather too many people, bumping into each other and chattering; the atmosphere is a little heady but Kevin does not notice this since all he is interested in is whether Jason is around or not. He is fascinated by Jason, who is more fun to play with than anyone else though also worrying. When Kevin is with Jason the world, sometimes, rocks a little.

He finds Jason and says, "What shall we do?" Jason ponders and decides that they will go down to the village and buy something to eat at the shop. Kevin casts his mind over his financial resources and works out that he has fifteen pence left of this week's pocket money. It is only when they are half way across the park that Jason thinks to dive in his jeans pocket and finds he has only two pence. They are distracted, however, from consideration of this problem by the sight of a rabbit, which they chase whooping to a ditch where it vanishes. At this point Kevin, struck by a thought, says "What 'ud we have done if we'd got it?"

"We'd have kept it for a pet."

Kevin is silent for a moment. He is a person dogged by reality. He says, "My dad 'ud have killed it and ate it".

Jason looks surprised and indeed a trifle shocked. "That's stupid."

Kevin frowns, trying to work this out.

At the shop, Kevin buys a Mars Bar. Jason, restricted in his choice, scrutinizes the trays of gob-stoppers, aniseed balls, lollies, mints and jelly babies in child-high trays along the front of the till. Above him, the shop lady serves another customer.

Jason, with a deft snatch, takes four gob-stoppers and pops them in his jeans pocket.

Kevin experiences a cold thrill in his stomach. He looks nervously upwards; the shop lady is still busy with till and customer. Jason is once more examining the trays of sweets.

The customer goes. Jason beams upon the shop lady and says can he have an aniseed ball please. The shop lady says of course you can my love. She beams back at Jason; two pence and an aniseed ball change hands.

Outside, Kevin says "You didn't ought to have done that. That's stealing."

"She didn't see," says Jason. He pulls a gob-stopper from his pocket, offers it. "Here you are."

Kevin hovers, hesitates, flounders. He takes the gob-stopper. "But it's stealing if she's seen you or not."

Jason sucks and reflects. "She's got lots of them."

Kevin gropes for an answer. At last he replies, "You can't just take things off of other people."

"But I wanted some," says Jason reasonably, "and I'd only got two pence."

Kevin gropes again. His mother prompts. "You can't always have what you want."

Jason, jovial, wallops Kevin across the back. "S' all right if you only do it sometimes."

Kevin, wildly confused, puts the gob-stopper in his mouth and then spits it out. It is a flavour he doesn't like. "The police could get you and put you in prison."

Jason, for an instant, is disconcerted. Then he says, "I'd escape, wouldn't I? I'd get over the wall with a rope."

Kevin, defeated, is silent. He wants, suddenly, the basic certainties. He announces, "I'm going back to our house."

"O.K." says Jason equably.

The small figures separate, at the cross-roads; Kevin to go to a cramped kitchen in which his mother will presently accuse him of getting under her feet, Jason to the perplexing freedoms of Framleigh. Neither looks back; each, almost instantly, forgets the other.

The course members, meanwhile, have assessed and discussed the domestic situation and taken action. It is agreed that in the interests of all, not least themselves, something will have to be done; reason suggests self-help. Keith Harrap draws up a rota: so many people to organize each meal, so many to lay tables, so many to wash up. Most – especially the younger members of the party – consider all this something of a lark. Honestly, says Jean Simpson, wait till I tell my husband, it's the bohemian life all right, isn't it? Sue says actually you'd feel a bit let down in a place like this if everything did run smoothly, wouldn't you? I mean, things being predictable all the time is so ordinary, that's what we're here to get away from. She looks over Keith's shoulder to see if by any chance she will be in the same duty group as Toby. But Keith, after some silent reflection, has left both Toby's and Paula's names off the lists. He could not say in so many words why he has done this, and hopes no one will draw attention to the matter; it just seemed, somehow, lèse-majesté – you simply could not see Toby washing a dish and Keith does not want Paula diminished by such activities. Happily, no one appears to notice.

The group responsible for getting lunch hasten to the kitchen to see what resources they have to draw upon. It is a quarter to ten and everyone is due on the terrace at ten to start the morning's activities. As it is, they will have to cut short their studio sessions in order to give themselves time to prepare the meal.

The kitchen, now, is tidy but the larder is unpromising. There is plenty of bread, and butter (though the butter is in fact margarine, as one or two people had already expected); spaghetti and packet soups and a fair amount of cheese and tinned stuff of one kind and another. The freezer yields a block of mince and a mass of stewing steak, which are taken out for later on. Eggs. Potatoes. Onions. The red-haired teacher, who has had experience of school camping trips, does some swift calculations and proposes a sensible and indeed tasty-sounding menu. Tasks are allocated for later, and the kitchen searched for things that will be required: pans, implements. While they are doing this they observe, through the window, Toby, Greg and Paula in the garden; Greg and Paula sit on a bench beside the path, Toby stands looking down, with that transitory stance he always has, as though he were only tenuously present, already half-departed for some more pressing and personal business. And indeed as they look he goes; whereupon Greg lays a hand upon Paula's thigh and the watchers, embarrassed, snap their gaze away, all together, and bustle once more in search of a tin-opener.

"Here we are," says the teacher, "not a marvellous specimen, but it'll do. Of course I imagine people like that are more relaxed in, well, in relationships, that sort of thing, than, than . . ."

"Than people like us?" says Keith, sharply. He, too, has seen the hand on thigh and has mixed feelings, none of them agreeable.

"But *are* Toby and Paula married?" asks Tessa. "I mean, nobody seems to know."

Keith, silent, slams potatoes into the sink. Tessa goes on to say that personally she thinks everyone should be creative in their lives whether they're artists or not and that means relating to other people in a creative way apart from anything else. She says this a little doubtfully since it is a theory heard for the first time last night from Bob, whose large confident relating arm was around her at the time. The teacher, who is old enough to be Tessa's mother, shoots her a suspicious glance and says well, I daresay, but up to a point. At which Tessa giggles and says you sound like my mum, which does not endear her to the teacher.

Keith, the irony of whose original remark has escaped everyone, is driven by exasperation to point out that he does not actually suppose Toby, Paula etc. to be a species apart. It's their life-style merely that's different, most of the rest of us have drives and emotions and impulses. The feel of the potatoes swirling in muddy water and the brisk domestic conversation of the teacher have pitched him back to his own Dulwich life-style, which he came here to get a break from. And indeed at this point Jason arrives at his side, one cheek ballooned out by a gob-stopper, and begins thickly to ask boring and unanswerable questions, bringing to mind Keith's own children who he dearly loves but at times would gladly strangle. Children he had not reckoned with, here. He dries his hands on a grubby dishcloth and goes.

Mary Chambers has wandered into the library, there being a few minutes yet before it is time to gather for the morning's activities. She is anxious to identify the daisy-like flower that springs from the cracks in the paving all over the terrace and paths. It's a daisy, isn't it? Paula had replied, on enquiry, but Mary suspects otherwise and searches for a flower book, to set her mind at rest. The library, however, a cavernous, dusty, echoing and unwelcoming room beyond the Common Room, is a disappointment, lined with row upon row of mainly empty shelves. Toby has sold off, over the years, any book to which value had accrued by virtue of age or rarity. Now, dog-eared paperbacks slide into thirties editions of H. E. Bates, Mary Webb, Michael Arlen, *Whitaker's Almanac*; a few bound copies of *Punch*; a Shakespeare; an incomplete Dickens; oddments of poetry; *Who's Who for 1939*; the *Good Food Guide* for 1964. No dictionary. Certainly no flower book. She glances through the paperbacks for a novel to read in bed, but there is little that she does not already know: old Graham Greenes, Evelyn Waughs, thrillers, a few fifties Pelicans. She leafs through Clive Bell's *Civilization*, a tattered copy, evidently well-read: Toby, at one time, was very taken with the idea of a leisured creative élite, so long as one was part of it, and indeed privately regrets that the ethos of today compels one to subscribe – at least out loud – to the notion of equality of creative opportunity. Mary stands for

56

a few minutes reading, a slight frown on her face. She is interrupted though, by the sound of voices. There is, unknown to her, a further door to the library, beyond a huge leather screen at the far end, and Toby and Bob have at this moment come through this, engaged in a discussion that does not sound entirely amiable. Mary pops *Civilization* back on the shelf and hastily retreats.

"Thirty per cent" says Bob.

"Look, Bob, there are four of us. Me, Paula, Greg, you. Right? You're pushing it a bit."

Bob grins.

"O.K., I know the potting's a big draw. But fair's fair. We've always split four ways. Actually Paula's always felt it ought to be shifted a bit more towards me since after all I provide the ambience."

"Some of us," says Bob, "have done a fair bit to ginger up the bloody ambience."

"All right, all right – you did a marvellous job on the studio and I appreciate it. You're a damn good carpenter – I wish I had the patience for that kind of thing myself. But thirty per cent – Christ, Bob! Look, I'll have a talk to Paula about it."

"You do that, old lad."

"It goes without saying," continues Toby, after the slightest of pauses, "that I tremendously value your contribution to Framleigh."

"Grand," says Bob. "That's all I wanted to know."

"There is always the possibility that I may one day be able to expand the whole Framleigh concept, in which case . . ." – Toby gestures, implying untold munificence – "But for the time being, as you well know, we're working within a very restricted margin. Frankly one is overwhelmed at times with the administrative hassles."

"Me heart's bleeding for you, mate" says Bob. "Think it over, anyway." And goes.

Potters, of course, are two a penny. On the other hand a potter who can also turn his hand to carpentry, the odd building job, bits of general maintenance, and whose bluff northern charm is a proven attraction, is perhaps another matter. Toby himself regrets the present Framleigh financial set-up, whereby the four permanent faculty split between them, as salary, whatever profit remains when the cost of running the courses is deducted from the cash they bring in. He would have preferred what he calls a more genuine co-operative system whereby there was some kind of kitty and he administered it, but somehow that idea has never appealed to the others. Paula can really be irritatingly middle-class about money and Greg was remarkably quick, Toby feels, to latch onto the fact that some kind of a share-out was in operation. If and when the Framleigh Foundation comes into being there will be an altogether different arrangement, which quite possibly will not include Bob, Greg or conceivably Paula at all.

"*Married* to Toby!" says Paula. "God, what do you take me for!"

The day being of such perfection, she has declared it would be a crime to stay stuck in the studio, and accordingly has taken her group outside into the park for some simple sketching. Corny, says Paula, but fun. Find something nice and textural, children, and draw away. Even the hackneyed old wild flower study I shan't reject. Right – back to the drawing-board!

Keith is trying an impression of the house from one side of the prospect, where he sits with Paula on a section of broken stone coping. Paula, from time to time, drifts off to oversee others of her charges and then returns to take up the conversation; this enormously gratifies Keith, though the drawing frankly is boring him – he had no idea a house had so many blasted angles.

Keith shifts uncomfortably. "Well, I imagined . . . Jason, after all . . ."

"Oh – Jason. Yes, Jason's Toby's of course. But the point about children is that they *are*, isn't it? Not *whose* they are."

"Mmn," says Keith noncommittally.

"I've had the marriage bit," says Paula, "absolutely and once and for all."

Reluctant to pursue this, Keith returns to the matter uppermost in his mind: the conflict between his own life and what he feels may be his nature. "Sometimes I feel like throwing it all up," he says, "and doing my own thing."

"Why don't you, then?"

Keith hesitates. "Well – money, security and all that stuff. It's a question of Karen and the kids really."

Paula shrugs.

"I mean, I know if I put it to Karen, of course she'd say do it. But it seems so selfish. You can't just think of what's right for you personally."

Paula, shredding a grass stem, stares at him. "You know, Keith, you're way off target there. You're missing the point. It's not a question of you, it's what you can do. Your potential."

"Oh, I don't know . . ." Keith begins modestly, but the reference, he at once realizes with chagrin, is to abstract potential, not to his in particular. To Paula's, in fact.

59

"I mean – what if I'd taken that sort of attitude when Philip – my husband that is but not any more of course – wanted me to rot in Maidenhead as a suburban wife and mum. Dinner parties for his friends, and his parents to stay twice a year."

"Well, yes" says Keith. "It would have been the most terrible waste. What did Philip do?" he adds, after a moment.

"He was a doctor. Still is, presumably. Oh, Christ, it was all just insane. I married him when I was nineteen – I mean, how could I know what I was going to turn into? So I had to duck out of it, didn't I? If I'd stayed there I'd have become someone else, someone I'm not. There'd have been no 'Introspective Woman', no soft sculpture, no mirror work, no 'Adam and Eve'."

"God . . ." says Keith, nodding. "I see what you mean." He frowns at his drawing, which grows more unsatisfactory by the minute. "Actually," he continues, "I wanted to ask you – I've been wondering about enrolling for a macramé course at the local poly. Do you think, um, do you think that would be a good idea?"

Paula pulls a face. "Hobby stuff," she says, "finicky."

Keith, chagrined, jettisons macramé. In fact, during the last year he has run through woodwork, photography and lino-cuts. Photography looked promising for a while and the developing process was satisfying, but somehow his photographs never really seemed artistic – just quite good photographs. Nothing he'd ever taken up had seemed right for him, so far. Poetry. That bloody novel. Writing was the most unsatisfactory of all; in a poem you never could hit on the right word and in a novel something had to darn well happen and the problem was what. Oh, ideas were easy enough – what the stuff was about, one's responses and all that – it was how to get it down and anyway it all took so long. Something much more immediate is his scene, he suspects.

He returns to the drawing, and finds that according to him the building slumps in the middle, not surely a part of Kent's original conception. Paula has gone; looking up, he sees her wandering down the prospect, striking a vibrant note against the bleached grass, in her long orange skirt and black top. The sun flames the windows of the house, so that it appears to be inwardly consumed by a raging inferno; the prospect rolls down into the Warwickshire fields; a gleaming aircraft with a snout like some probing insect slides up into the sky and swims across the view, roaring. And all around, on the terrace and along the woodland rides and by the cascade and the serpentine rill, people are hunched over drawing-boards, turning nature into art, trying to impose order upon chaos.

Chapter Five

"What are they paying, dear?" asks the novelist's wife, rattling the car over the Framleigh cattle-grid.

"Nothing."

"*Nothing!*"

"I know, I know. I did murmur about usual arrangements and so forth but he's evasive, this Standish chap. The trouble is, I've always rather wanted to see Framleigh."

"It could do with having its avenue re-surfaced," says the novelist's wife. "This isn't doing the car any good. God, what's that thump?"

"A stone. I say – there's the house. Rather nice. It's the park that's the great thing, of course. He did at least mention dinner."

"I should certainly hope so. Thirty miles, on a wet night!"

Framleigh, revealed suddenly and with a flourish as the road twists, looks more appealing and indeed imposing at this distance than it will do in close-up. From here, the grand design of things is to be appreciated: the closing of the perspective to draw the eye towards the house, the grouping of trees, the use made of contours, the careful manipulation of nature. The novelist wonders how far Kent's original tree planting survives. His wife, swerving to avoid a pot-hole, asks which particular spiel he is going to give them tonight. The contemporary novel? The writer's craft? One is tempted, says the novelist, given the setting, to hold forth on the eighteenth century and the picturesque, but I daresay that might be presumptuous – presumably Standish himself is capable of doing that. I suppose in the end I'll just do a reading and then something general.

"He's a painter, did you say? I haven't heard of him. Or does he paint under some other name?"

"I don't think so," says the novelist. "No, I can't say I have either."

The course members are assembled in the Common Room, awaiting the something rather special arranged by Toby for tonight, Wednesday night. Several people have been mildly disappointed when this is announced as a visit by Richard Waterton, the writer; they had hoped for something a bit more dashing. Someone talking doesn't sound all that exciting, and most of them have never even heard of him. One or two of those who have had thought he was dead anyway; Tessa, learning that he must be seventy plus, loses interest in the evening altogether and torments herself trying to summon up courage to wander nonchalantly over to the studio and see if Bob is around. Mary Chambers has read several of Waterton's books, and explains that they are rather intellectual novels but – this, with diffidence – actually she has enjoyed them. Sue, the librarian, who has not

63

read Waterton but has frequently shelved him, points out that he is that old-fashioned kind of writer who also produced in his time poetry and books about other books. Short stories, too, someone else remembers. Greg, who was not consulted about the invitation, says that frankly Waterton is not spaced out, as a writer, and his stuff is way back so far as literature is concerned but he sounds a nice old guy.

Toby, as it happens, has not read Waterton either but he has seen his name from time to time in the Sunday papers. It is in this context that he has invited him. Waterton, evidently, has an interest in eighteenth century architecture. An article by him on the Adam brothers appeared recently in the *Sunday Times*; it was rather heavy going and Toby merely skipped through it but it struck him that Waterton might be the man to do an appreciative piece on Framleigh, the strategic appearance of which in something or other would do no harm at all in connection with his telephone conversations with the man in London. Accordingly, he looked Waterton up in *Who's Who* and found that he lives in the same county.

The car draws up outside the house. Waterton and his wife, getting out, study the façade and their faces fall a little. I didn't realize, says Waterton, about the Victorian addition. Wow, says his wife, look at the greenery growing out of the gutters. And I say that attic window's got wartime blackout stuff on it still, surely? The accretions of time, says Waterton, appropriately picturesque, I suppose.

The front door being open, they enter, hesitantly. The sight of Paula's sculptures in the marble niches of the entrance hall stops them in their tracks. At this moment Paula herself appears, and graciously welcomes. She takes in Waterton, who is a plump and stumpy figure, and his wife who is no beauty and wears a Marks and Spencer's cotton dress, and the welcome is tinged with patronage. Gracious patronage, naturally. Come, she says, everyone's agog, and Toby's about somewhere – ah, here he is.

Toby comes rapidly from the Common Room, with outstretched hand. I loved your last book, he says simply. And now come and meet people and have a drink. I thought maybe a quick look round the place before we eat and then after dinner everyone's dying to hear you, does that sound a good arrangement?

In the Common Room, the Watertons are temporarily quelled again by "Adam and Eve" and the fiery effect of Paula's ethnic cushions and covers. Waterton, a number of thoughts passing through his head, goes to the window and looks out at the terrace and the prospect. He cheers up. Ah, he says, now the cascade and the serpentine rill are off to the right, are they not? I remember the plans in the Soane Museum. And the temple will be somewhere beyond those trees. Toby opens the french window and the party moves out onto the terrace. The rain has stopped and everything steams a little. Waterton, looking down, says happily, oh, how nice, that little erigeron daisy, one doesn't often see that. Mary Chambers, close by, says with interest that she'd thought it was an erigeron but hadn't known which. *Erigeron mucronatus*, says Waterton, an introduction of course, not native, it naturalizes when it likes the soil. I wonder, Standish, might we nick a root or two before we go? Me too, says Mary, I'd been going to ask; she and Waterton exchange looks of approval.

"But it's a weed, surely?" says Paula.

"Even weeds," says Waterton with a smile, "have names."

"Oh goodness, I can never be bothered with all that. It's like being back at school, learning lists of things."

"A rose is a rose is a rose," says Mrs Waterton. "That would be your approach?"

Paula glances rather more sharply at Mrs Waterton; there is an edge to her tone that surely isn't possible from someone who looks like that. Paula tosses her hair back over her shoulders and wades in her long Indian print skirt through the clutches of the erigeron. The group assembles at the edge of the lily-pond, and stares down into it.

"You ought to get that Japanese pond-weed out," says Mrs Waterton. "It's smothering the water-lilies."

Greg points. "It's full of bugs – look at them all."

Waterton peers into the pulsating waters. "Bugs? Oh, I see what you mean. Water-boatmen, snails, too. And there's a caddis fly."

"You people," says Greg kindly, "really are into terminology, aren't you?"

Waterton, straightening, looks at him. "Well, it's a small way in which one can impose order on an otherwise confusing world. Children get rather keen on it, at quite an early stage, I've noticed. Wouldn't you agree?"

"It's science, basically" says Greg, "isn't it? I find myself reacting against anything scientific. As a poet."

Waterton opens his mouth, but his eyes meet those of his wife, across the teeming pond, and he closes it again. After a moment he says, "We'd love to see the rest of the park, wouldn't we, dear?"

It is indicated to the course members, by Toby, that the conducted tour of the park is a matter for the Framleigh faculty only. No need, he says, for the rest of you to get your feet soaking, and they drift back into the Common Room where one or two head for the decanter of sherry which had arrived to greet the visitors; this, though, has somehow disappeared.

The Watertons, flanked by Toby, Paula, and Greg and followed by Nick, move down the prospect, stand for a moment to look at the view and have the temple pointed out to them, and then turn into the woodland way, where, in the distance, "Introspective Woman" glints in the orange sunlight that shines now from crevices in the rain-clouds. Waterton says that he seems to remember early prints of the park in which an Apollo stood here, and Toby explains the departure of the Apollo and goes on to remark that most people love the spatial relationships created by the present arrangement and the way it gives a jolt to the visual sense.

Mrs Waterton remarks that that is an interesting way of putting it. She observes that Henry Moores, in an outdoor setting, do that too. Though, she adds, the effect is rather different. Paula looks again at Mrs Waterton, dumpy in her cotton dress, hugging an anorak round her shoulders; she cannot understand why such a drab little woman should make one feel somehow uncomfortable.

They visit the cascade and the rill. Waterton is happily enthusiastic, though dismayed at the rampant decay all around. He makes sympathetic sounds in response to Toby's account of personal struggle and self-sacrifice in the interests of a heritage; Mrs Waterton says little but appears to listen. Greg and Paula fall behind, talking. Nick trails at Toby's elbow. When they turn off the woodland way into the path to the grotto, passing the site of the stinkhorns, he becomes nervously chatty, and is put down by Toby, who is still outlining to Waterton his schemes for the rehabilitation of the park, if only it were possible.

They reach the clearing and stand admiring the view, a sweep of Warwickshire transformed by the golden evening light into a scene of pastoral nostalgia in which the eye is caught only by the spire of a church, a line of surviving elms crowning a hill.

Waterton fills his pipe, evidently in a state of comfortable appreciation. " 'Consult the Genius of the Place in all . . .' "

"I was afraid," says his wife, "you were going to say that." Her feet are now very wet and she has snagged her tights on a bramble.

"Sorry, dear" says Waterton mildly.

"Is this where that old guy fell on a rock?" asks Greg, approaching.

Toby explains, to the Watertons, that there was a tragic mishap yesterday in which one of the course members was injured. "Mercifully he seems to be recovering nicely. I gave the hospital a ring just now."

Mrs Waterton enquires for how long the courses have been going and Toby, in replying, outlines briefly the Framleigh ideal. "A possibility for artistic withdrawal," he says. "For us, of course, but for the ordinary people who come on the courses as well. That is how I like to think of it. A creative sanctuary."

The Watertons, listening to this, move a little closer together, as though imperceptibly closing ranks. Mrs Waterton appears to forget her wet feet and Waterton tamps his pipe with a very square and unaesthetic thumb. He says, "I see. You feel then that the artist requires social detachment?"

"The artist," says Greg, "has to alienate himself. Freak out in every way. Intellectually. Emotionally."

"And what, then, is he or she going to be artistic about?" asks Mrs Waterton tartly. " 'The proper study of mankind . . .' " She glances at her husband and suddenly grins. "My turn . . ."

Waterton lays a hand on her arm, but addresses Greg. "Well, that's always been a point of view, but I must say I prefer involvement myself. Both for creative purposes and as an artistic responsibility. Whatever that awkward term may mean. Mind," he adds, turning to Toby, "I speak as a writer. I suppose there is a difference. But I would have thought the painter also . . ."

Toby is wearing his burdened look. He stares into Warwickshire and says, "The artist's responsibility, so far as I am concerned, is to himself."

"I'll say," snaps Paula, *sotto voce* but nonetheless drawing a quick glance from Mrs Waterton who announces that if nobody minds she is getting a bit damp and should they perhaps rejoin the others back at the house.

The duty group has been busy in the kitchen. Dinner, when it is served, is not too bad, in fact. The Watertons tuck into onion soup, macaroni cheese and tinned fruit salad. They chat pleasantly to members of the course. Mary Chambers, with great diffidence, asks a question or two about Richard Waterton's novels: she has noticed that he always seems to bring in gardens and gardening and has wondered about this. She is reluctant to use grandiose words like symbolic but somehow manages to do so and finds that it is quite all right; she doesn't feel as silly or out of her depth as she had expected. What Waterton has to say in reply is most interesting, and leads on to a more mundane but equally engaging conversation about the merits of various works of reference on plants. All in all, Mary has a good time.

Keith Harrap sits next to Paula, who seems uncharacteristically subdued. He notices for the first time how much attention Paula pays to her own person: she is forever adjusting it in some way – smoothing her hair behind her ears, caressing neck or breast, running a hand over the contours of her face. She is a very good-looking woman; it is as though she needs the reassurance of her body to confirm that she is really herself.

"We have had," says Toby, "a bit of bother over the staff situation. But everyone has rallied round wonderfully."

Tessa, who has an arrangement with Bob so far as the rest of the evening is concerned, is restive, with one eye on the clock.

Sue, by now, is in such a state of sexual tension and frustration that she is permanently a-twitch. She fidgets and judders and when Toby comes anywhere near she suffers an internal fever that is much the same as having a high temperature. Toby, who is well aware of this, and well aware also – since in some respects he is not totally impervious to the human condition – that the sexual drive of women is quite as strong as that of men (his own, as it happens, is rather low) is amused. Occasionally he panders to his amusement by giving her a smile across a crowded room, or brushing against her as he passes. He could put her out of her misery by taking her to bed at some point, but he probably will not bother; he has other things on hand just now. She has managed to sit herself next to him at dinner and spends the meal alternating between ecstasy and distress.

"God," Paula says to Keith, "the last thing I want is this bloke holding forth on his boring books. Heaven knows what Toby thought he was about, asking him to come."

Keith, nervous that the Watertons may hear this, glances up the table, but Waterton is talking to Toby; in an attempt to calm Paula he remarks that actually he hasn't read any of them and wonders if she has. "I never have time to read, do I?" says Paula petulantly. Keith agrees that he too finds it difficult to fit in.

Waterton, who has come to look more and more strained as the meal progresses, is asking Toby, politely but with perhaps a certain absence of involvement, if it is possible to keep Framleigh economically viable by means of the Study Centre. Toby sighs. He indicates, in his reply, frustration and self-sacrifice, hints at official philistinism and obtuseness. "One has tried," he says, "just about everything. I need hardly say that the Arts Council in its great wisdom has never seen fit to give Framleigh a grant." Waterton looks noncommittal, but Mrs Waterton appears to choke slightly on her fruit salad. Sue says hotly, "That's a shame". Toby lays a hand for an instant on hers; "You're sweet to say so. The truth is that it's exactly what one would expect, the world being the way it is."

The meal over, everyone goes through to the Common Room, where coffee is produced. The Watertons are both, by now, restive. Waterton disappears to the lavatory where he has a swig at the emergency flask in his raincoat pocket; he is not, in the normal way of things, a heavy drinker, but long years of literary life have taught him that there are certain associated trials for which it is necessary to be prepared and this evening is clearly going to be one of them. Slightly restored, he rejoins the others.

It is decided that the reading should be got under way. Waterton is installed in an armchair at the side of the fireplace, and, after a few introductory words, starts to read an extract from one of his early novels. He plans to follow this up with something from the most recent and then try to make a few points about development of style and technique. The audience settles.

Mrs Waterton is so placed that she has no option but to contemplate "Adam and Eve". She tries looking sideways but there her attention is caught by a huge Moroccan bedspread which is used as a hanging, suspended by some kind of tasselled fixture from Kent's cornice. A naturally tranquil person, rational so far as it is possible for anyone to be completely so, she feels quite disordered by this place. Mild irritation has already given way to some more serious malaise: she would rather like to be violently rude to someone which is not a thing she often is. She closes her eyes, seeking the reassurance of her husband's voice.

At this moment all the lights go out.

Bob, over in the studio, has just handed Tessa a can of lager. He stands over her in the darkness and reflects that circumstances can occasionally be most remarkably accommodating.

Jason, upstairs in bed, opens his mouth and yells. He continues to yell for two or three minutes and then starts to pad downstairs, exhilarated now rather then distressed.

Waterton halts in mid-sentence. There are rustlings, the odd giggle. Paula exclaiming "Oh, Christ!" Toby gets up, says "I suggest people just stay put. Nick, give me a hand with candles."

Toby and Nick are gone for quite a while. Conversation breaks out. The night is dark beyond the uncurtained windows, so there is nothing to be seen but the suggestions of bodies dispersed around the room. Someone, getting up to grope for an ashtray, falls into someone else's lap and there is much hilarity. Waterton attempts one or two light remarks and then gives up. Mrs Waterton sits morose and silent.

Jason potters across the hall and into the Common Room. He can't see properly so he decides to crawl on his hands and knees so as not to walk into anything. He will find Paula and make her jump. There are lots of people sitting in chairs in the Common Room and it is difficult to know who is who. He crawls around legs, and finds a promising pair.

Mrs Waterton feels the shaggy head of some dog pressed against her calf, about, she senses, to bite. In her jangled state this is the last straw and she cannot stand dogs anyway: she lashes out with one foot. At the same instant Toby appears in the doorway shooting the beam of a torch ahead of him, there is a howl, and Mrs Waterton sees that she has clouted a small boy wearing nothing but the bottom half of a pair of pyjamas. Her own childlessness makes her possibly rather more susceptible to children than most people: she gets up, uttering a kind of moan, pushes past Toby into the hall and heads for the cloakroom.

Toby and Nick have not been able to find any candles. There should be a more than adequate supply in the store cupboard; there is always a supply, the Framleigh wiring system has not been renewed for forty years and this kind of thing has happened before; but there is not a damn candle in the place. In fact, Jason borrowed the candles some time ago when he had a den in the woods in which he was going to camp out. He has long since forgotten this, or indeed the existence of the den. So there are no candles and only two torches. Toby curses; Nick flutters in distress.

Jason howls, and is mollified by various people. Waterton, bewildered at his wife's sudden exit, follows her from the room and finds her in the darkness of the cloakroom. "The best thing we could do," she says, "is get out of this madhouse." Waterton, himself unsettled and irritable, snaps that they can hardly do that. He makes use of his flask; Mrs Waterton takes it from him and says that if that's the situation she'll join him.

The Watertons, now a little heady, go back into the Common Room. One of the torches has been placed in the hall, providing a circle of light which does not reach very far. The Common Room is still in darkness and people are getting restive. Toby and Nick are now inefficiently searching the fuse box for the trouble; they replace various fuses, to no avail. Eventually they return and Toby announces that the bloody system seems to have conked out altogether and he has called the electricity board, who promise assistance before too long. He suggests that Mr Waterton should continue from where he was so rudely interrupted.

Waterton, by the light of the other torch, reads. But darkness has done something to the composure of the audience; there is now the disquieting stir of an unruly schoolroom. Someone mutters, and gets responsive suppressed laughter. Greg says something not quite audible that induces more laughter. Paula yawns loudly – though of course there is no telling from whom the yawn comes. Waterton becomes flustered and reads the same bit twice. He cuts the reading short before he had intended. At once Greg's voice is heard. "That passage you repeat, is it some stylistic effect you're after?"

"What passage?" asks Waterton, and then, irritably "Of course not, that was a mistake."

"I beg your pardon" says Greg, "I thought we were into the *nouveau roman*." He, too, has been bolstering himself with alcohol (that private bottle of scotch) and his usual extreme politeness has given way, disconcertingly, to something close to aggression. "If you don't mind my saying so, the piece doesn't have much thrust. It's draggy. Maybe you could do something with the dialogue."

Waterton finds that he does mind Greg saying so, quite

74

extraordinarily much, in fact. A tolerant man, in the normal way, he has been reduced either by Framleigh or the unaccustomed use of the flask to thumping rage. "As it happens," he begins, "the piece as you call it has been in print now for a considerable time, incorporated in a novel which some of my readers are kind enough to consider . . ."

"Excuse me," says Greg, "I thought this was something you were trying to get published. Forget it."

Waterton, who for many years has not so much tried to get a book published as despatched his next work to an expectant editor, swallows, carefully and deliberately. He selects words, aware that dignity requires precision, but before the words can come out Toby has broken in to remark smoothly that personally he loved that descriptive passage and to ask if anyone else has a question to put to Mr Waterton.

"Actually," says Paula, "I'm interested because I used to write myself once though I never had time to finish the novel I was working on. Is the man in the book you?"

Waterton abandons the words he had selected and chooses others. Paula's response is wearyingly familiar. He starts to speak but is interrupted by a shuffle and crash from the back of the room. One of the course members has complained of the room being stuffy and Keith Harrap, moving to open the window, has tripped. There is a confusion of apology and exclamation and the torch is borrowed from Waterton (who takes advantage of his relegation to darkness to have a swig at the flask, which he had had the forethought to put in the pocket of his jacket). "Sorry," says Keith Harrap, meaning it.

"Oh dear," says Mrs Waterton, "do let's get on."

She sounds petulant, and Waterton, taking up again his reply to Paula, has a pomposity and a defensiveness that was not there before. It is as though Framleigh has had the effect of disordering personality: Mary Chambers, observing this, sits in the gloom and reflects. Paula and Waterton are now engaged in an argument in which Paula's observations are so maddeningly insubstantial as to drive Waterton, attempting response, to apparent sarcasms which are alienating his audience. Restiveness spreads.

"Well, I don't really see what you're getting at," says Paula. "I just know as an artist that creativity is sort of from within. I mean right you learn method and so forth but the actual nitty-gritty, the real . . ."

"Oh, shut up!" says Mrs Waterton.

Jason, who is sitting on the floor under the big table, watches this with interest. He is quite used to hearing grown-ups talk thus – he has after all spent all his life with Paula – but he senses, with a child's intuitive ear, that the comment is out of character. Disorder appeals to Jason.

"Shut up, shut up!" he chants, from his lair. Sue and one of the other younger members of the audience giggle.

Waterton gets to his feet. "I really think . . ." he begins. Something has happened to his voice: it is slurred, more from anger than the effects of the flask but the impression given is unfortunate. He starts again "To be quite frank I don't feel that there is a great deal of point in . . ." Someone in the audience – Jean Simpson – gives a little hiss of disapproval. It is one thing for people like Toby and Paula to be unconventional, but an elderly man like that . . .

Toby also rises, and says things about maybe it's getting late and our guests . . . Jason is still chanting shut up, loudly. Sue and her neighbour are killing themselves. Mrs Waterton walks out into the hall. Other people start to talk. Paula cries well, for God's sake, all I said was . . .

*   *   *

Outside, the Jaguar driven by Sir Henry Butters, Chairman of Harpers Bank, slides to a halt in front of Framleigh. Sir Henry and his wife stare in perplexity at the building, from which no lights shine at all. The night is not quite black, since a half moon lurks somewhere behind cloud, which makes the unlit bulk of Framleigh even more disconcerting. "Are you sure . . ." begins Lady Butters, but at that moment a light is seen to waver across one of the large downstairs windows and from within comes a gust of sound, the sound of voices, rather loud, raucous voices. The Butters look at one another. "I think," says Sir Henry uncertainly, "perhaps we had better come back another time. I understand from Jacobson they're some sort of artistic colony." Lady Butters gives Framleigh a look of alarm, and nods in agreement. The Jaguar beats a hasty retreat into the night, passing on the avenue a Midlands Electricity Board van.

A quarter of an hour later, the Watertons' car also leaves, at a smart pace. Mrs Waterton drives, hunched over the wheel. Neither Waterton speaks until, at the entrance to the park, Waterton says "There's the most awful smell of petrol, dear, had you noticed?"

Five miles further on, at the side of a deserted road, the Watertons, on all fours, stare at the underside of their car, from which petrol issues in a fairly steady stream. Mrs Waterton recalls, through clenched teeth, that she had remarked on a bang from somewhere underneath when they approached Framleigh. It has started to rain once more.

Chapter Six

Jason stands at the end of a bed in which are Bob and Tessa.

"Push off, mate" says Bob amiably.

"Why's she got no clothes on?"

"Because she was too hot. Hop it, there's a good lad."

Jason contemplates them. "I haven't got anything to do."

"Well, I have. Come on, hop it."

"You don't like me, do you?" says Jason, after a pause, in injured tones.

Bob sighs. "I think you're great. Just at this minute I want to have a talk to Tessa."

"What about?"

"This and that. Look, there's some cash on that table. Why don't you take twenty pence and toddle off down to the village shop and get yourself some ice-cream?"

Jason reflects. "O.K. Thirty, though."

"All *right*" says Bob sharply.

"Why's her face all red?"

Tessa gives a kind of moan. Bob sits up violently. "Bugger off, Jason. Right?"

Jason picks up forty pence from the table and walks to the door with dignity. He turns round and says, "Anyway you shouldn't smoke cig'rettes in bed. I can see the ends in that ashtray. There's notices about fire rules in all the bedrooms. I'll tell Toby on you". He goes out, banging the door.

Out into the bright Framleigh morning, empty as yet of anyone else, both faculty and course members being as yet either at breakfast or slowly rising, recalling with degrees of surprise the curiosities of the previous evening. Jason, for whom the evening was neither here nor there and is now in any case of no further interest, wanders into the anarchic world of the woodland way, bright with sun and leaf, active from the teeming undergrowth to the tops of the swaying trees. He is without plan or purpose – this of course distinguishing him from the life by which he is surrounded, most of which is busy either eating or being eaten. He pauses to investigate a dead pigeon, an ants' nest, a hole in a dead tree. He is bored as only a child can be bored, drifting from one distraction to another; he ploughs through time like someone walking through water. And the day is uncontrollable, as are all days, so far as he is concerned it might go on for ever, time is chaotic, unreliable, it expands and contracts like elastic, already he has lost his bearings and cannot remember if the next meal is breakfast or lunch. He ponders this problem for a moment, then abandons it to follow a speckled butterfly that is wavering around his knees. He echoes the butterfly's apparently purpose-less flight up and down Kent's woodland ride until it arrives at the plant for which, perhaps, it had been searching. It settles, and Jason squatting, examines it. Its wings have an intricate pattern of cream spots and its body is powdered with golden fur.

Jason perceives that in some way this is marvellous, but the thought does not form itself into words; he simply absorbs the butterfly, amid the humming morning.

The course members, being mature and ordered people, unlike Jason, are quite clear about the time of day. Some of them are complaining that breakfast is twenty minutes late, and casting aspersions on the efficiency of those on kitchen duty this morning. And the tea is stewed, at that.

The truth is that most of them are a little out of sorts this morning; their equilibrium is disturbed. Last night's atmosphere hangs still in the Common Room, seedy as stale smoke. There is a feeling of things having in some way got out of control, of people behaving in ways they would not normally; Sue remembers giggling at that really rather nice old man, who reminded her faintly of her grandfather. Keith, in that disorienting darkness, had at one point laid his knee against Paula's adjoining knee: what he cannot now decide, and the uncertainty is demoralizing, is whether what he took to be an answering pressure may not have been merely Paula shifting position in the stress of the discussion. Everyone has a sense of the subtle turning of the tables upon the Watertons, who had seemed initially such sane, almost reassuring, representatives of what several still think of as the ordinary world. Although of course Richard Waterton was – is – himself an artist, of a kind, which confuses the matter.

Tessa is silent, inwardly burning with a mixture of shame, anxiety and excitement. It isn't that she has not been to bed with anyone before, actually there have been three – well, two and a half, sort of – but this was different. She hadn't realized people actually . . . The night returns, and she bends scarlet-cheeked over the cornflakes.

Mary Chambers is thinking about Framleigh: not its physical manifestation but its capacity for . . . for somehow upsetting people, discomforting them, engendering conflict. And that of course stems not from the place but from its occupants though there is a curious sense in which the house and the park are a demonstration of this: the jarring apposition of the harmony and order of their conception and the muddle of today. She thinks again, with a twinge of doubt, of Toby's "little talk" on the first night; "doing your own thing" is of course an expression one hears a lot these days. A lot of people seem to feel it is a good idea. Observing, last night, the disintegration of the Watertons, she felt uneasily that the Framleigh atmosphere included a corrosive substance – corrosive of the personality. People, here, tended to behave not quite like themselves, as though some lurking aspect of the character got, for a while, the upper hand. You could tell the Watertons weren't really like that at all; that business after the lights went out was ridiculous.

Toby is irritable. Waterton, clearly, hadn't exactly been on the Framleigh wave-length; not that the power failure helped, of course, or Paula and Greg being so bloody argumentative, but the thing was a wash-out anyway. No point in bringing up the subject of an article in one of the Sundays. He does not appear for breakfast, but drinks tea in the kitchen, after a barbed exchange with Paula. Subsequently, another line of thought leads him to the gun-room, where he spends some time finding out the telephone number of the Saudi Arabian Embassy.

There is a row – superficially genteel, but a row nevertheless – between Jean Simpson and one of the other women about the duty rota. Some people feel they are doing rather more than their fair share. In fact the real world – the world of washing-up and negotiation and expedient behaviour – is impinging more than anyone had anticipated. Curiously, no one blames this on the Framleigh people; it is felt, still, that they can hardly be expected to cope as adroitly as others with that kind of thing. They were let down by the Filipino girls.

It is, now, Thursday morning, and one or two people remark on this, noting that it doesn't feel like it and how nice not to be on the way to work, or already at it. In fact, the three days of the course have already produced such a sense of suspended time that what day it is seems neither here nor there, Framleigh being above or beyond such mundane tetherings. This must be the life, sighs Jean Simpson, just getting up in the morning and doing what you want to do, day in day out. She is reproved by Keith Harrap, who points out that what is done is work the same as any other. Artists work. Well yes, of course, she says, I know that, what I meant was . . . Her voice trails off. She gives Keith a nasty look. I didn't mean what they're doing isn't serious, don't get me wrong, just it's . . .

Nicer, thinks Mary Chambers. Oh yes, much nicer, surely? Her own day, at this time, would be a tumultuous but planned and indeed orderly process of getting people off to school and the house cleared up and herself into the car and on the road for the polytechnic where she works three days a week as part-time secretary in the administration office. She quite likes the job but it is not, of course, in the last resort, interesting. When people ask her what she does and she tells them they say oh yes, and there is a silence. Quite often. Presumably that does not happen to Paula. Or to Toby or to Bob or to Greg. This has never, in fact, bothered her much; she is as interested in her own response to others as theirs to her, though the responses tend to be private. When Mary does not like someone they usually remain unaware of the fact. She wonders, occasionally, if she is too passive a person. But passivity implies absence of feeling, and Mary has feelings all right. It is simply that she does not normally express them; she cannot remember when she last shouted at anyone, and the nearest she comes to a display of ill temper is heightened colour. "It's good that you're expressing yourself more," her sister said recently, looking at her paintings; exasperation turned Mary crimson.

No, she does not envy the Framleigh people exactly; besides, they are different from most people she knows or has known and envy is reserved for those most accessible, on the whole. She does, perhaps, envy their capacities, their artistic capacities. And yet . . . She thinks of Greg's poems, which are all about Greg. And Toby's suite of lithographs called "Personality studies" which are not of people at all but are elegantly coloured distributions of spirals and loops and coils. And Paula's soft sculptures and chicken wire creations and her mirror things which do indeed look quite difficult to do but don't somehow add to your vision of anything except possibly old tights or chicken wire or pieces of broken mirror.

Keith, having put down Jean, is feeling slightly disgusted with himself. Ever since he came here he has had this tendency to be snide with people which is not the way he normally is except towards one or two colleagues who damn well ask for it. But Jean is a perfectly agreeable woman, if unoriginal. Keith telephoned his wife late last night, and knows in retrospect that he wasn't very nice to her, either, and for no good reason except that she mentioned some problem with a blocked drain. Just at the moment he doesn't want to know about things like that. His irritation with Jean is of course because he himself had been thinking much the same thing, but in his case envy of the Framleigh life-style is mixed with uncertainties about his own. What if he did chuck it all up? What if he went home to Karen and said right, we're off to Majorca or Cornwall or wherever, I'm getting out of the rat-race, I'm going to see if I can make out in hand-crafted furniture?

On the terrace, awaiting Toby with his clip-board and the morning's distribution process, the group is quiet, preoccupied along these lines, and others. Jason, emerging from one side of the prospect, sees them as unavoidable and perhaps unfortunate furnishings of the place; they interest him rather less than the more unpredictable and entertaining aspect of Framleigh – the infinitely flexible landscape, to be made into what you will, given the time and the imagination, both of which Jason has in plenty. Jason has no fixed concept of the world: nothing it produces would surprise him. People do not much surprise him, yet. The natural world is not so much surprising as a marvellous and manipulable convenience, there for his personal benefit. Like others at Framleigh, he sees everything in terms of its relation to himself, but Jason, of course, is not yet grown-up.

The group disperses; the terrace is once more empty. Jason wanders up the prospect, climbs the broken bit of the balustrade and squats beside the lily-pond. He observes its fervent life; things that wriggle and things that crawl and others that scoot to and fro across the surface, a striving disordered soup. The Japanese pond-weed, at the moment, is winning. Jason takes a twig and chivvies a water-boatman, to see how fast he can make it go.

Nick, in a corner of Toby's studio, is doing some clearing-up chores; he often finds himself doing that kind of thing. Not, of course, that he minds: to be at Framleigh and with Toby under any circumstances is better than not to be at Framleigh at all. At least so he supposes, uneasily; from time to time he rather wishes he had never met Toby in which case he might perhaps have found a job by now and be, well, settled, instead of in a state of perpetual insecurity and apprehension.

His position at Framleigh has never been defined. Sometimes he is invited to share Toby's bed and at other times he is not. When he goes home, to the mother in Reigate with whom, theoretically, he lives, Toby never enquires when or if he is returning. When he does return Toby may be apathetic or warmly welcoming, there is no telling which.

Of course, in fact, he is incredibly lucky to have met Toby at all, that he does realize, and it is very silly and faint-hearted to feel otherwise: all emotional experience, surely, however upsetting, is better than no emotional experience?

He met Toby eighteen months ago in the gallery near Victoria at which Neil Burton, who taught Nick at college, had an exhibition. Nick had helped to hump pictures from the studio to the gallery and as a reward was invited to stay on for the private view and there suddenly was Toby, being awfully charming and friendly and interested and, as he left, laying a hand on Nick's arm and saying look if you're ever up our way drop in at Framleigh and tell me what you think of my things. Nick had been stunned when Neil Burton, grinning sardonically, had told him that Framleigh was by way of being a stately home and Toby really rather grand. Watch it, though, young Nick, he'd said.

The first few times at Framleigh he hadn't known much about Paula; she'd been away staying with someone in Spain. Of course there'd been "Adam and Eve" and "Introspective Woman" and the soft sculptures but he hadn't really given them much thought – there'd been too much else to think about. And then the next time there she was, and Jason, and she scared the wits out of him. "Is it all right me being here?" he'd asked Toby. "Paula won't mind?" And Toby had looked amusedly at him – "Why should she, Nick?" As though, Nick realized, blushing and chagrined, he were assuming a status he very evidently did not have. Thus could Toby give with one hand and take away with the other.

Nick is helping out, insofar as he has an official status. "My assistant," Toby occasionally describes him as, to course members. He does the things that nobody else has the time or the inclination to do, such as tidying the studios and sending off brochures to people enquiring about the courses and checking on supplies of everything from paint and paper to drums of cooking oil and cartons of detergent. It is a pity he can't drive or he could take over the trips to the Cash and Carry from Greg. Greg he finds less alarming than Paula, but equally disconcerting; he has a knack of making you feel – well, kind of ignorant and uninteresting. Once, there was a conversation about poetry and Nick said he liked Philip Larkin and Greg roared with laughter. He patted Nick's shoulder and said, "You go right ahead then, Nick, just carry right on."

Greg is supposed to have published this collection of poems, with a rather special small publisher in New York, but somehow there are never any copies at Framleigh.

And now Nick, stacking paper and reflecting upon the previous evening, out of sorts and with a feeling that Toby is annoyed with him, thinks with a little spurt of venom that Greg was disgusting to that old man. Going on at him like that. Rude. Paula too. Of course, there wasn't anything Toby could have done, really, but . . .

*   *   *

86

Toby and Paula meet half way across the stable-yard. Toby has left his group in Nick's charge while he goes in to make a couple of phone calls; Paula is bored and having a breath of fresh air.

"Last night," says Toby coldly, "was a balls-up."

Paula retorts that he was asking for it, bringing a couple of stuffy old things like that along.

Toby observes that Richard Waterton is a very well known writer.

"You've never read a word he's written," says Paula. She has the unique privilege of ten years' intimacy with Toby and speaks, hence, with authority; Toby, knowing this, gives her a look of tempered hatred. He does not really hate Paula, being in fact incapable of extreme emotion of any kind, but just at the moment he doesn't much care for her.

"Neither," he says, meeting her on her own ground, "have you."

"I never said I had."

Toby changes tack; he knows only too well how long this kind of thing can go on. "Greg overdid it. Frankly if he throws himself around like that again I may have to reconsider his position at Framleigh. It's the sort of thing that gives us a bad name."

"Greg may be going back anyway," said Paula. "Actually I may go over with him for a bit." She has grave doubts as to the truth of any of this; the remark is a tactic rather than a statement.

Toby also has the advantage of ten years' experience of Paula; she might well, he knows, take off for a while but the odds are that she will be back. She always has been. Greg, on the other hand, is less predictable and as it happens Toby rather wants Greg around for a bit longer. He does actually pull his weight at Framleigh and he has done a good job over the last year or so at

87

keeping Paula amused and therefore preoccupied. Paula when bored and hence restive is inclined to poke her nose into areas of Toby's life which do not bear close inspection.

"I'm merely suggesting that Greg should be more careful about chucking his opinions around when we have these sort of occasions. As it happens I very much appreciate Greg's contribution to Framleigh; I'm simply making a small criticism about handling visitors."

Paula eyes him suspiciously, trying to work out the meaning of this swerve.

Toby looks at his watch. "Christ – nearly eleven. I've got to make some calls." He wipes a worried hand across his brow. "Look, has anyone checked the stores? The lot who're doing the cooking today are in some sort of tizz about food."

"I suppose I'll see to it," says Paula, and stalks away across the cobbled yard.

The cobbles are broken and, in some places, missing altogether and where there are gaps a carpet of camomile has spread – an unusual growth and a survivor perhaps from another age of Framleigh. Paula treads the camomile with sunburned feet clad in thonged sandals with black tapes that wind around and around her ankles and calves. She has handsome legs. She wears today a short denim skirt and a red silk shirt with the top two buttons undone. She has handsome breasts, too.

Once upon a time, Toby and Paula loved one another. Up to a point and in so far as either was prepared to give way to an emotion which does make great demands on egotistic natures. Over the years, love or its equivalent has shrivelled (both have found alternatives for that, in any case) and the relationship now rests on self-interest, a capacity with which Toby and Paula are both healthily endowed. They find each other convenient.

The camomile, crushed by Paula's passing feet, fills the yard with its scent.

Keith Harrap, who is spending the morning in Bob's studio, happens to look up and so sees Paula's silk and denim back view disappear out of the yard. Since he has been thinking of Paula this causes a disconcerting twinge, as though lust had made her manifest. Not, of course, that what he is feeling is lust, precisely, though he is perfectly aware that – to put it baldly – he fancies her. No, the thing about Paula of course is not just that she is such a good-looking woman but that she is such a talented and interesting one. If she looked like the back of a bus she would still attract him (though not admittedly in quite the same way).

Paula disappears. Keith goes back to shoving clay around, rather half-heartedly. He thinks of Karen, his wife. He transfers himself to the kitchen at Dulwich, where Karen is getting lunch for the children. He considers her, with total detachment. At least, no, not that, because the image of her brings with it unavoidable accompanying feelings of . . . of, well, familiarity and yes, love and knowledge and various kinds of tolerance. And a maddening twinge of concern about the blasted drain that, she is quite right, will have to be seen to.

Mercifully, this unsatisfactory line of thought is interrupted by Bob announcing that it is time to down tools and go over for some nosh.

"Are you sure you don't mind?" says Paula. "Driving's one of the boring things I've never got around to doing."

Keith runs through the gears of the minibus and adjusts the

89

mirror. He doesn't mind at all, as it happens, though come to think of it there is something a little curious about jumping with such alacrity at the chance of an expedition to some supermarket.

Paula delves in the pocket of her skirt. "Where's that bloody list? The thing is, Greg's stuck into a recording session and he just can't risk losing the creative drive by breaking off."

Keith nods sympathetically. Actually, his response to Greg has been growing more negative by the minute, these last couple of days; he could well be, Keith suspects, a right jerk. Poet or not.

"And apparently we're cleaned out of just about everything. Christ! Domestic hassles – how I loathe them!"

"Not to worry," says Keith. He swings the minibus masterfully over the ruts of the Framleigh drive.

"Right," instructs Paula. "No, I meant left." Keith reverses the minibus into a gateway, a trying operation. He is reminded, just for an instant, of his mother who has the same irritating inability to give directions. He glances sideways at Paula's long tawny hair, hanging over her red silk shoulders, to reassure himself.

Paula puts on a pair of very large sun-glasses that swamp the upper half of her face, and talks. She talks all the way to Woodbury, where the supermarket is, and of course what she has to say is fascinating, being all about (or mostly about) art – her art, specifically – and the doing of it and how it makes you feel and what the hang-ups are. Not everything relates directly to art – some of it is more specifically about Paula herself – but in a sense that is neither here nor there, since, as Paula says, art is what she is for, quite simply. Once or twice Keith puts in a comment but these never really get taken up; sometimes it is as if Paula did not hear and at others she digests the comment into

90

what she is in the process of saying, so that it seems to turn into something different. Talking to Paula is like talking to someone with a heavy cold: her sensory responses are curiously muffled.

The supermarket is as other supermarkets. And yet, of course, it is not, because to tour it in Paula's wake, trundling the trolley and stowing into it the items plucked from the shelves and flung back by Paula, is an interestingly heady experience. Heady because Paula makes it so, stalking down the aisles tall and contemptuous, manifestly slumming, manifestly above this kind of thing. Eyes follow her; the eyes of ordinary Woodbury housewives. And move from her to Keith, in his safari jacket, a bird of the same feather. There are no other men of his age in the store: they are all in offices or on building-sites or in factories or selling things to other men. This is freedom, of a kind.

Paula drops a pack of lagers into the trolley. "I'm parched. We'll stop and have a drink on the way back." At the check-out, she stands while Keith and an assistant stow the purchases into carrier bags, and then, as an afterthought, finds a cheque book in the pocket of her skirt. She has, Keith observes, the most enormous handwriting, great loops and swirls that entirely cover the surface of the cheque. He wonders, madly, if she might ever write him a letter.

It is quite a haul getting the bags back to the minibus. Keith does two journeys and Paula does one, bearing the lightest of the bags. In fact, she does not have to carry it all the way as a bloke suddenly appears offering to help; it is interesting that while Paula is neither frail nor elderly there is something about her that makes people – some people – feel instinctively that such a person shouldn't have to do things like lug heavy shopping.

They set off back to Framleigh. On the way, there is also the bank to be visited and a builders' merchant where Paula gets putty and off-cuts of mirror and other tools of her trade. By the time they have finished the expedition has taken a couple of hours, the afternoon is well on, and Paula says again that she is parched. "There's a place we can stop off on the way. A sort of ruined church thing."

The ruined church, Keith recognizes at once, is in fact a monastic building, the shreds of an abbey. He has always had rather an interest in architecture and likes to look things up and put names to this and that. The abbey, what is left of it, crumbling and shrouded in greenery, agreeably unpreserved, the archetypal ruin, looks to him thirteenth century though he spots the ghost of a romanesque window in one wall and the massive stump of an early pier. He mentions this to Paula, who stares at him, and says the texture of the stone is gorgeous, and as a matter of fact she used it as the model for some rather intriguing ceramic work last year.

Beyond the ruins, away from the road, is a grassy space. "Let's sit," says Paula. Keith opens two cans of lager. The sun comes out. "Heaven," Paula lies back. "God, what an afternoon! You were an angel to help, Keith."

It is the first time, he realizes, that she has used his name and simultaneously, she reaches out and pats his hand – a warm, disorienting touch. The view of Warwickshire swings a little.

He glances briefly sideways. She has rolled up the sleeves of her shirt and pulled the neckline back, to get the sun. Her eyes are closed. His own hand rests like a leaden weight upon the grass, a couple of inches from her thigh. He swallows. Things are getting really rather rough.

"You know, Framleigh does have the most extraordinary effect. I don't know when I've felt so . . . so, well . . ."

"Liberated?" murmurs Paula.

"That's it," says Keith gratefully. He lifts his hand, and puts it down again. Paula shifts, rubbing her back against the grass. Keith shifts also, uncomfortable in various ways.

All of a sudden Paula sits up. "Christ . . . There's something inside my shirt!" She flaps her hands wildly behind her back, then yanks the shirt from the waist of her skirt. "Oh God, what is it?"

Keith investigates Paula's bared back. There is nothing to be seen except skin, a single elegant mole placed off-centre left of the spine, and the straps and fastenings of a lacy black bra. He reports.

"I felt something crawl," says Paula, "I know I did."

"Well . . ." Keith begins. He takes a breath. He reaches round her and puts a hand on her breast, the fingers under the rim of her bra.

"Hey!" says Paula. She sounds amused.

She turns round. She looks surprised but in no way offended. "What's all this about?"

"I thought . . ." Keith begins, stiffly.

"Oh, God, did you?" says Paula. "Oh no, there really was something crawling. But look here, if you're feeling like that . . ." and she puts a hand firmly on his crotch. "I never like the idea of anyone suffering in silence. And I like you – you've got a lot of hang-ups but basically you've got a lot going for you."

Keith looks round wildly. There is nothing to be seen or heard except birds, insects and distant traffic. He says, in disbelief and surging hope. "Here?" Things are pretty well unquellable now, in any case.

"O.K." says Paula, amiably. She undoes her shirt.

The couple, appearing suddenly from round the side of the abbey, are elderly and inclined to tweeds. The man carries some kind of guide-book. They glance towards Paula and Keith, nod and smile. Paula does up her shirt again in as leisurely a way as she had undone it.

The couple peruse the exterior of the abbey. The man produces a camera and there is a lot of fuss about taking some pictures. They have some kind of discussion and then sit down, fifty yards or so away. Sandwiches are brought out.

Paula gets up. "That" she says "looks like that. Christ – look at the time, anyway. I've got to clear up the studio before the evening session."

Walking back to the minibus behind her, Keith sees something on the sleeve of her shirt. Moving. It is a small furry brown caterpillar. He reaches out and flicks it off. Paula says, "What's the matter?"

"Nothing."

They drive back to Framleigh. Paula talks, about much the same kind of thing as on the outwards journey. Keith drives too fast, in a state of painful diminishment.

Chapter Seven

At the moment when Keith is examining Paula's bared back Toby is in the gun-room at Framleigh putting a call through to the man in London. He has already had a conversation with someone at the Saudi Arabian embassy, the second over the last couple of days, which has not been particularly satisfactory. He is passed through switch-boards and secretaries and achieves, eventually, the clipped tones of his quarry. He mentions one or two points he forgot during their last conversation.

"Our chairman and his wife happened to be in your area last night," says the man in London.

Toby makes sounds of regret. "They should have dropped in."

"They did. It seems the place was in pitch darkness and there were funny noises coming from inside. At least that is what I have from Lady Butters."

Toby contemplates, for a few moments, the ceiling of the gun-room. "Experimental theatre has become something of a feature of the Centre's activities. I envisage – once the expansion programme gets properly under way – a permanent stage in the new workshop area and of course the appointment of a Drama Fellow."

"Fellow?" says the man in London. "I see."

"The kind of thing, of course, to which your organization's name could be attached. The Harper Fellowship."

"I see," says London voice, again.

Toby doodles on a pad: a decorative arrangement of spirals and arabesques. "I should perhaps mention that my financial advisers are in favour of an adjustment to the figure we were talking about last time."

There are discreet murmurings, down there in London. "I'll be free in half a minute, Mandy. In which direction, Mr Standish?"

. "Downwards," says Toby. "We might be talking of, er, one million three. That sort of thing."

"Well," says the man in London, "this could remain an on-going conversation, I suppose. But before we go much further there should be a high-level inspection, I feel. We may come back to you on this, Mr Standish. Goodbye and thank you for calling."

Toby hangs up. He studies, for a moment, a framed photograph of his father and some other men, slung about with guns, standing amid the heaped carcasses of birds. The walls of the room are indeed lined with such photographs, some of them of considerable antiquity. Toby, whose awareness of the cash value of age is perhaps even more highly developed than that of others, reflects upon the commercial possibilities of these, and makes a mental note.

Sue, Tessa and Jean Simpson, packed into Mary Chambers' mini, drive into the north Cotswolds for the afternoon. They plan to have a look at one or two of the villages and generally potter around. Nice, says Jean, to have a bit of a break from the rarified atmosphere. She sits in the front with Mary and talks about her husband's promotion. Sue and Tessa, in the back, think their own thoughts: Tessa is riven by the worry that she might be pregnant and the marginally greater worry that Bob has said nothing about meeting tonight; Sue is busy despising Jean Simpson and determining that never never will she get like that. She will never marry a man in frozen foods and have two children and a pin money job and a part-share in a holiday flat in Newquay. She will, eventually, meet a man who is uncannily like Toby and live with him somewhere abroad; he of course will be involved in something creative and she will help him with it. She will grow her hair long and have a permanent sun-tan and never go near Coventry for the rest of her life.

Mary Chambers drives along sinuous roads through a landscape in perpetual movement, a kaleidoscopic sequence of scenes: field rising to tree-crested hill, cottage glowing in the sun, black and white cows brilliant against the green. Colours dissolve before her eyes as light ebbs and flows – from gold to fawn, from blue to grey, from the ink-dark of stooping summer trees to the brilliance of new grass. Nothing stays the same; the visual world, which should be the one stability, slips away as foxily as time itself. The spire of a church rises apparently from a cornfield, poppies flare at the roadside, rooks beat their way from horizon to horizon.

"Pretty country," says Jean Simpson. "You could get past that lorry now, there's a straight bit coming up. Sorry – back-seat driving."

They arrive at a small market town. "Touristy," says Jean. "Let's stop and have a poke round, all the same. The shops look nice."

The place is clogged with cars. Cars crawl in search of parking spaces, hover at likely spots, double-park while their occupants, safely glassed in, stare fixedly ahead. The old market square, now the central car park, is full up. Mary cruises round once, then again. Jean spots a car backing out; Mary, advancing, arrives at the empty space at the same moment as a woman driving a Jaguar. "Oh, quick . . ." says Jean. The cars halt, wheel to wheel. The woman gesticulates. Mary's passengers stare, grim, at the elderly man and girl in the Jaguar, who glower back. The two cars sit; if either advances they will graze bumpers; behind, someone hoots. "Look at her blue-rinse," says Jean, "don't give in, Mary." Mary, too, feels a surge of resentment; the woman, beyond her window, is mouthing something. The car behind hoots again; Mary says desperately, "We can't just go on sitting here"; Jean stabs with her finger at the Jaguar – "We got here first" she mimes, as to the deaf. And the Jaguar, suddenly, shoots backwards, the driver glaring. Jean says, "There! It's always just a question of holding out." Mary, feeling cheap, drives into the parking space.

The town is full of people: the contents of all those cars, of course. It is doing good business, which since that has always been its *raison d'etre* is perhaps not so inappropriate as some might think (Jean, for instance, who continues to deplore the crowded pavements). Business, though, nowadays, is in batik from Indonesia and woven table mats from Korea and jeans made in Hong Kong and Spanish pottery. Very few of the things sold are necessities of life; it would be quite hard to find a loaf of bread.

Tessa buys a see-through muslin top (made in India) and Sue a jar of wild rose, elderflower and honey conditioning cream. Jean lingers over Japanese paper kites – dragons and serpents and exotic birds – but decides they are too pricey and anyway the kids would have them ripped up in five minutes.

They find themselves in an art gallery selling pottery and

prints. The pots, they agree, are not a patch on Bob's; Tessa does not join in the discussion but stares at the pots, throbbing. The prints are gaudily abstract affairs of blobs and spirals (though entitled "Thames Valley Studies") and prompt Jean to remark that they remind her of Toby's things. Sue says violently that they aren't a bit like. Jean stares again at the prints and then, coolly, at Sue and suggests that that is a matter of opinion, perhaps. Mary, promoting harmony, asks Jean if she likes Toby's work.

"Well, I mean, they're brilliant, of course, aren't they . . .? But I s'pose not, really, since you ask. I mean, I wouldn't want to have one – put it that way".

Sue, icily, interjects. "They cost seventy-five pounds each, his lithographs."

Jean, at once impressed by the sum and annoyed by the implication that hence they are not for the likes of her, is silent.

"What about Paula's sculptures?" asks Mary.

"She trained in London and on the continent," says Jean, after a moment. "It says so in the brochure. And she's had exhibitions. Mind, I think they take a bit of getting used to, but they do sort of grow on you in a way. And of course she's such a personality. She's got such style."

Mary points out that that on its own wouldn't make her a good artist. Jean concedes that this is so, but frowns. Sue, who appears now to be joining ranks with Jean says, "Everyone at Framleigh's different from ordinary people. That's what makes it all so special."

Jean agrees that they are certainly different. "More free and easy, I suppose, is what it is. And they don't sort of take much notice of each other, do they? They all do what they want. Mind, I do think that child is let run wild, and I've yet to hear him said no to."

Mary wonders if not taking notice of other people is a necessary part of being an artist. The woman in the corner of the gallery, behind the cash desk, looks at her, and then attends to a customer. Half a dozen pottery mugs are wrapped up, and the cash register records the sale. The woman is wearing a brown smock, floor-length; you can see she is not just a shop assistant.

They emerge from the gallery. Jean and Mary would like a cup of tea; the girls decide to have a wander round. Tessa longs to confide, but cannot bring herself to do so; they talk about jobs, and holidays, and Sue's jar of conditioning cream, thinking, both, of other things.

Jean and Mary, who have nothing in common but their age (forty-two) enjoy a Cotswold farmhouse tea and talk, a little warily, of families, of jobs, of whether or not Jean should buy for her husband a batik tie displayed in the restaurant which sells, apart from tea, a few tasteful products by way of fabrics and home-made jams. Jean decides not to buy the tie. She tells Mary about various other weekend courses she has attended; an ornithological one, last year, was interesting. The ornithologists, too, were a bit of a law unto themselves, though not in quite the same way. The tea has encouraged candour; she eyes Mary and wonders if she, too, finds that however super your family is you need to get off on your own occasionally? Mary, noncommittal, murmurs. Jean sighs; "I wouldn't half mind," she says, "being Paula. Put myself first and no nonsense. But you've got to be doing something special before you can do that, haven't you? Nothing special about booking dental appointments all day, is there?"

Mary replies, thoughtfully, that people need to have their teeth seen to. "How do we know," she goes on, "that what Paula is doing is special?"

Jean frowns, again. She busies herself with a fair division of the bill and says eventually that well, we don't really, I suppose, but she is an artist, there's no getting away from that, is there?

They meet, the four of them, at Mary's car. The time limit for parking is about to expire; at a lamp-post's distance lurks the traffic warden, whom they have beaten by a minute or two. "What a job . . ." says Jean. "I ask you . . ." From the passenger seat, she gazes at the traffic warden, who gazes stonily back. Mary reverses the mini into the square, turns again towards Framleigh, and they travel once more through landscapes that compose and re-compose themselves around them, as relentlessly fluid as days, as thoughts, as moods. They sit side by side; what they say and what they think seldom coincide. Jean and Mary talk about a place they both know in Devon; the girls discuss a film. Jean is deciding to get a new kettle like one she spotted in a window just now; Mary wonders how to paint the flight of shadows across a hillside; Tessa does not so much think of as experience Bob – his hands, his voice, his smell; Sue tells herself a story in which she and this man she is going eventually to meet who is so uncannily like Toby are arriving in the south of France – no, Italy – and buying for themselves this gorgeous old farmhouse place in which they are going to live. And work.

Jason spends the afternoon at Kevin's house. He watches, with interest, Kevin's mum make a cake. When the afternoon telly programmes begin he sits, transfixed. Kevin's dad comes home for his tea and Jason, loitering, gets himself included at the family table. With that chameleon talent of childhood, he takes on the flavour of the background: he sheds Framleigh and assumes the style of the village. The difference, to him, is apparent but not significant: thus also birds live in trees and do one thing and fish in ponds, doing another.

Framleigh, by the early evening, has filled up once more. The doors onto the terrace are open; people wander in and out. Mary Chambers sits by the pond and watches its teeming life; she is thinking still of the tea-table conversation. Keith Harrap sits with her, reading the newspaper he bought in Woodbury. He does not wish to dwell on the afternoon's events and retreats with a certain relief into an account of political malpractice in Bangladesh. In the kitchen, those responsible for the evening meal are bickering; the initial panache has rather gone out of self-catering. Toby sidles in at one point and murmurs things about what a grand job they are making of it; there is perhaps the very faintest note of resentment in the response of some to this.

Paula has a bath. Greg comes in and talks to her while she has it. His recording session went, apparently, very well; he hit a fantastic creative streak. Paula, hearing this, feels excluded and hence grumpy; personally, she says, she had a hell of a boring bloody afternoon.

And as the shadows lengthen down the prospect people gather again in the studios, and make things.

"Art," says Greg, "is cathartic. It's got to be." He has had a session with the scotch bottle before supper, in celebration of a good day's work, and is in fluent discourse at his end of the table. Jean Simpson nods sagely. Greg pursues this theme throughout the first course and on into the bread and cheese that follow it.

After supper, a group leaves in the minibus to go to the

102

cinema in Woodbury, where "Midnight Cowboy" is showing. Bob has volunteered to drive them. Of those who are left, several opt for an early night. The rest sit over mugs of Nescafé in the Common Room. Greg, unexpectedly, produces the scotch bottle; morale, after a while, lifts appreciably and Keith, vanishing to his room, returns bearing, somewhat sheepishly, a further bottle – secreted, it is evident to all, against hard times.

After ten minutes or so Paula says, "Let's *do* something. I'm fed up with sitting around talking."

"Let's play a game," says Jason hopefully. He is in his pyjamas but shows no inclination to go to bed, nor does anyone propose that he should. His suggestion, though, does not go entirely unheeded. After a few frivolous offers, it is decided that liar dice might be amusing. Greg has dice. The table is cleared of mugs and magazines; Greg, Paula, Keith, Mary Chambers, Nick, Sue and – after a moment – Toby, gather round it. Sue and Mary Chambers do not know how to play. Greg explains. "The scoring is like poker, right?" – both shake their heads regretfully and further explanations are necessary – ". . . but then the point is that you lie. O. K.? You keep your hand over your dice and you tell the truth about how many you're throwing but nothing else. You call true or false – whichever you like – and pass on the dice to your neighbour, calling higher than the previous call – only he or she knows if you told the truth or not."

Jason, who is to play in tandem with Paula, grasps this principle with ease; Mary and Sue are bewildered for the first couple of hands and inclined to run scared. Mary, passed by Paula two jacks and assorted rubbish which are alleged to be a full house kings high, panics, claims four aces which are challenged by Greg and is eliminated. She experiences a small gush of irritation.

The hand continues until only Paula and Toby are left. Paula takes a swig of her whisky, gazes at Toby with an expression of exaggerated innocence, "Four queens, my love. Four beautiful queens. Look, there's two of them."

"I'll see them all," says Toby, expressionless.

Paula sweeps the dice together. "Blast you."

"Trial round," says Greg. "The kitty stays." Two pence is the agreed stake. Toby's face flickers.

Toby wins the next round also. He continues to play impassively, curving his hand tightly over the dice and frowning down at them.

Jason enters into the spirit of the thing with enthusiasm. A daring hand starting at full house, unspecified, proffered by Paula travels the table until it founders at Sue. "We're best at lying," says Jason proudly. "We're gooder at it than anybody."

Toby wins again. Coins accumulate, now, on the table.

Sue is pink with the excitement of it all. She is so close to Toby that their knees collide, from time to time, under the table.

Greg turns to Keith with narrowed eyes. "I'm giving you three kings, jack and nine. Take it or leave it."

Keith has so far been eliminated with his first call, each round. Last time, Paula said "Oh, ducky, you've got to play rougher than that." He considers, says "O.K." and receives a fistfull of junk. His attempt to pass on full house, kings on nines, fails.

Greg wins the hand.

Paula peers down at the dice. "I've got two queens and, um, two tens and an ace. No I haven't – I've got *three* queens and a ten and an ace." She gazes blandly at Nick.

Nick hates liar dice. The game is often played at Framleigh. He always loses. Losing he does not mind; it is the curious implication of failure that goes with it. To be good at liar dice is an odd skill. Toby is very good at liar dice.

"No," he says, after a moment. Paula lifts her hand triumphantly.

Toby wins another round.

Sue looks archly at Toby. "You'll never believe this, but I've got three tens. And a queen and an ace."

"I'll take them," says Toby. She watches his face as he receives just that; there is not a flicker. He studies the dice and Sue sees to her astonishment the cushion of his little finger move ever so slightly, tipping one over. She wonders at first if he has not himself noticed what he did, and then if this is a refinement of the game that has escaped her. After a moment she realizes that it is not; she blinks uncertainly. Toby passes on, according to him, three tens and two queens, and that indeed is what he has, as Nick discovers.

Coins have accumulated. Toby has lots, Greg a few and no one else any.

"Liar! Liar! Liar!" chants Jason.

Mary Chambers is getting better at the game; she is aware of this and, like Nick, of the curious concept that better at it is what you get. Worse would seem the more correct term. She wins a hand.

Greg wins the next, and in the ensuing one he and Toby are left in confrontation, Toby claiming four kings which on the face of it looks improbable; Greg declines this but before Toby can reveal the truth or otherwise someone's unwary movement tilts the table and the dice slither to the floor. "Damn," says Toby, retrieving them, "have to scrub that one." "Ooh," says Jason, "who kicked the table accidentally on purpose?" "Yes, quite" says Paula. "*What* a pity."

Greg says nothing. He gives himself another tot of whisky.

Nick now has a nasty feeling in his stomach. When first he

started coming to Framleigh there was a craze for croquet; one of his earliest memories of Paula is a snapshot of her croquet mallet raised to hit Toby after Toby had swiped her ball into the undergrowth at the side of the prospect. Toby usually won the croquet games; on the occasions he didn't he would contrive to bring things to a premature end, loping back to the house on unspecified errands. Toby prefers winning things to not winning things; so do most people – the difference being that Toby seems to mind awfully, which is odd when you think what sort of person he is really. It has always worried Nick just a bit, this. Once, he and Toby played Junior Scrabble with Jason and Toby got in a temper because Nick played the sort of concessionary game that would allow Jason to win; Toby did not.

Keith and Greg each win a round. Jason counts the coins on the table and announces that Toby no longer has more than anyone else. Jason is much enjoying himself; he circles the table looking over people's shoulders.

Greg plays a really dirty game, Keith thinks; an odd reflection, on the face of it, given that that is the general idea.

Paula is becoming snappy.

Mary Chambers finds to her surprise that she too is getting cross when foiled; particularly, for some reason, when foiled by Paula or Greg. She is playing, now, to win.

Toby and Paula are left confronting one another. Toby accepts from Paula three kings, ace and jack. Paula stares at him in triumph; "Gotcha," she says. "Possibly," Toby replies politely. He studies the dice. His other hand holds his whisky glass, empty; "I wonder . . ." he says, to Keith. "Oh, sure" says Keith. He gets up; people shift their chairs to let him out of the circle. Toby's finger once again, Sue sees, nudges over one of the dice.

Jason surfaces suddenly behind Toby's chair. "Ooh!" he cries

106

happily, "he knocked his dice over. Now he's got two aces. He's not allowed to do that, is he?"

"I'll say he isn't," snaps Greg. "Hey . . ."

Toby's face remains inscrutable. "Isn't it," he remarks, to the table at large, "about time that child went to bed?"

"Did he honestly?" says Paula to Jason.

"Yes," says Jason blissfully. He skips from foot to foot. "Toby cheated! Toby cheated! People oughtn't to cheat, ought they?"

Sue, now, is crimson, but no one notices. Nick, too, is in a lather; he did not quite see what happened, but experience of Framleigh has given him an intuition as to truth and falsehood. He thinks Jason, who frequently does not, was probably telling the truth.

"Christ," says Paula conversationally, "how childish can you get . . ."

The side of Toby's face twitches: a dangerous sign, to those who know.

"Well," says Greg, "frankly that's the last time I . . ."

Keith, returning to the table with two filled glasses, stumbles over a leg shot out in his path by, in fact, Nick. The whisky goes everywhere. "What the hell . . ." says Keith angrily. "Oh, gosh, *sorry*," says Nick. "I didn't see you . . ." He mops the table feverishly with a wad of Kleenex; the dice, now, go everywhere. "Oh, for heaven's sake . . ." says Toby. "This is becoming a shambles."

The cinema party, returning at this moment, come into the Common Room to find the place reeking of whisky and everyone either sullenly silent or snapping at one another over a heap of two pence pieces. In front of the fireplace, benignly observed by Paula's appliqué-work Adam and Eve, Jason squats on the floor throwing dice. "Five aces," he cries. "Cut my throat and hope to die. Five lovely aces, take them or leave them."

Chapter Eight

Mary Chambers lies awake. She has not, tonight, telephoned her husband. Her last call was unsatisfactory: "Power failure?" he said. "Richard what? Who? I'm sorry, Mary, I don't quite follow who all these people are." And she found herself, irrationally, snapping: he should know, it shouldn't be necessary to give laboured explanations, he should take things in. "I don't know," she said, "where the spare fluorescent tube for the kitchen light fitting is. If Steven has lost his cricket sweater I don't see what I can do about it from here. And I can't tell yet if I am getting something out of the course or not. No, I am not irritable, I am just saying I can't tell. No, dear, there isn't anything wrong and yes, the other people are nice. Most of them are nice. Some of them are nice. There is a rather nice little boy."

The truth is, she has realized, that no one at Framleigh can teach for toffee. Bob can get you to make a pot that is reasonably functional, if not a work of art. The others have strong opinions, but that is not enough, in a teacher; teaching requires a certain personal detachment, and that quality is not in good supply at Framleigh.

Artists, Mary supposes, have heightened perceptions; they are like the rest of us but more so. They see more; they feel more; they have the gift of expression. Certainly feeling and expressing are done at Framleigh, but whether feeling and expressing of a different order than in the world beyond is a matter of opinion . . .

Admittedly these are not great artists; no one is saying that. And how *they* go on goodness only knows since one has never met any, nor likely to. In fact, Mary reflects, there is a sense in which you could expect a real artist to behave better than other people rather than the same or worse. If there's any truth in the idea that artists are different – that they are capable of things the rest of us aren't capable of, in seeing and understanding and being able to make other people see and understand. But just like creative people are expected to look different – though nowadays everyone looks like that, what with long hair for men and long dresses for girls – so they are expected to behave like creative people too. It is as though people couldn't be sure they were artistic otherwise.

She is feeling, she realizes, at odds with herself. Which is why she cannot sleep. Four days at Framleigh have caused internal displacement of some kind; a sprain in the mind.

Others, too, rest unsatisfactorily. Nick, who would have wished to offer comfort to Toby who is in a foul temper, is rebuffed and mortified. Keith is suffering intense sexual frustration compounded with other discontents. A number of people have indigestion brought on by the inadequately cooked spaghetti that was had for supper. Sue keeps reviewing, in perplexity, the liar dice game. Greg and Paula quietly wrangle:

"Kiss me," instructs Paula. "No, not there . . . *Here* . . ." Greg responds with a list of his own requirements. "Oh, all *right*" says Paula, "but fair's fair . . ." Greg tells her that she is not always into participation, in bed. "That's rich!" says Paula indignantly, "coming from you."

Jason, out cold, wrong end up amid a swirl of bedclothes, roams the forests of the night, at large in a mythic world of sensation. He pursues, and is pursued; he flies; he swims; he is the centre of the universe; only he is real.

Various people, waking, resolve that this is to be a day of decision.

"Look," says the red-haired teacher, thumping the Common Room notice-board. "One, two, three, four, five. I have done one duty more than almost everyone. I did supper last night and I'm on again for lunch washing-up. I don't know who worked this out but I don't call it right."

Keith, defensive, points out that the number of course members is not conveniently divisible; a few people (including himself) have to do extra turns.

"What I don't get," says someone else "is why the faculty aren't on. I mean, I don't really see why they shouldn't be there too."

Opinion, now, divides. There are those who still feel that you can't really expect this and others who have come to think differently, in some cases rather strongly. Keith himself sees no

110

reason why that jerk Greg shouldn't turn a hand. He hesitates. At this moment the telephone rings in the gun-room and, since it continues to ring and there is no sign of any Framleigh people coming to answer it, he goes. A crisp-toned man is asking for Toby; he leaves a number.

None of the course members like one another quite as much as they thought they did on first arrival. The friendship that looked about to blossom between Jean Simpson and the red-haired teacher has foundered over use of the shared bathroom on the first floor. Sue is suspicious of Tessa because once Toby laid a hand upon her arm. There are creative rivalries; people look over other people's shoulders not just to see how others are getting on but also to see how they are getting on themselves. This is actually part of the Framleigh Ideal and is called community interaction but it doesn't entirely work like that. Keith, although he has no objection to Mary Chambers, is privately humiliated because he sees that her rendering of the exterior of the house, done during Paula's sketch class the other afternoon, is greatly superior to his own. This shouldn't be the case: Mary is a pleasant enough woman but not, frankly, someone you'd take for artistic. She doesn't often open her mouth, apart from anything else.

Most people do not analyse all this but simply have a vague and slightly discontented feeling that they have not been as thoroughly detached from ordinary life as they would have wished.

Keith, fretfully waiting for a go at the bathroom, records that he has so far experienced irritation, lust, frustration, dislike, contention, jealousy and boredom. He could get all that at home. Curiously, though, he does not feel that this reflects on Framleigh so much as on him. He is basically loused up in some way. He sits on the edge of the bed, intently firming the decision that he made during the night. So much so that he does not hear the bathroom door open, and allows someone else to get in.

Toby, in the gun-room, dials the number on the slip of paper handed him by Keith. The number is, in any case, familiar. "Toby Standish here," he says, and, after a few moments, "By all means. No, quite convenient. No – absolutely no trouble."

He puts down the receiver and stands for a moment, wearing that burdened look. He wipes a hand across his forehead and pads out into the hall.

• Discontent, this breakfast-time, is apparent. Not universal, but festering here and there – around the red-haired teacher, who is still mulling over the matter of the duty rota, and around Jean Simpson who is pointing out that there is not enough cereal for all unless people hold back rather more than they are doing. There has been a rush on the only brown loaf, and those who have been unsuccessful are making do with toast from the sliced white loaves hurled into the supermarket trolley by Paula. Paula herself does not appear until most people have left the table; then, she sits in a white towelling bath-robe, drinking tea and looking morose. When someone approaches her to ask about marmalade she gazes at them for a moment blankly, and then sighs. "Oh God," she says, "there should be more somewhere. Why don't you have a hunt around in the kitchen." The questioner, made to feel importunate and mundane, backs away. Paula, washed now by a shaft of sunshine from the window, holds her cup in both hands and closes her eyes; she contrives to

112

look both exotic and deprived, as some goddess rudely prised from her natural setting and forced to suffer in exile.

Keith, coming in at this moment, hovers, but Paula's eyes remain shut. "Looking for something?" says Jean Simpson. He mutters, and departs.

Nick meets Toby coming from the gun-room. Toby pauses. he smiles – that warm, occasional, engaging smile. "Ah," he says, "there you are." He lays an arm across Nick's shoulder and steers him through into the library. "A word in your ear. Just that a little problem has cropped up . . ." Nick, his heart thumping, his shoulder alight, allows himself to be steered.

Tessa, up in her room, anxiously consults her diary. By the end of next week she will know if she is or she isn't. And if she is? Oh God, if she is . . . She licks her lips and runs through, in her head, the telephone conversation. She picks up the phone and tells all and from the earpiece comes Bob's friendly relating Yorkshire voice, saying . . . She stares at the diary and tries to hear what he says. And fails. He does not say anything; the number is unobtainable.

Sue, strategically placed at the long refectory table so that she can see Toby as soon as he comes in, observes Paula. Oddly enough, Paula has not that much interested her, hitherto. Even the question of whether or not she is Toby's wife has not seemed crucial. Paula, so far as Sue is concerned, is a creature from another planet. Paula does not take the bus every morning from Stivichall into central Coventry; Paula does not stamp books, day in day out, book her holiday in January, wash her hair on Tuesdays and Fridays, worry about whether she has thick ankles. Paula strides around Framleigh all the year long, creates, wears fantastic clothes and, presumably, goes to bed with Toby. All of which is inconceivable, or well-nigh so. Nevertheless, at this moment Sue furtively studies Paula: her handsome face turned to the sun, her thick tawny hair, her long shiny sunburned legs folded one over the other, the bath-robe falling back from them. It isn't fair, Sue thinks, it darn well isn't fair; there is absolutely no reason why she should not be Paula, and Paula her. Never before – or never much – has this kind of resentment hit her. She is neither particularly discontented, nor particularly covetous, in the normal way of things. On the whole, she usually feels, things aren't too bad as they are; life is acceptable, and what else can you expect? But this morning, sitting in the Framleigh refectory (where Kent's original cornice still runs around the room above the trestle tables and the benches, the Nescafé and the cornflakes, hinting at another ambience) it is not quite like that. One or two adjustments in the scheme of things and she might not be where she is, doing what she does; she might be – well, not Paula but someone not too unlike her. Toby, of course, is a special person and in a sense unapproachable: he really is different. But Paula, over there on the other side of the room, admittedly on the sunny side, does not, suddenly, seem like a person on another planet; actually, in this light you can see that her long brown legs need shaving.

Greg glances into the refectory and passes on through the Common Room and out onto the terrace; he doesn't feel like breakfast, in any case, or at least not a lousy Framleigh breakfast. There are some things the British do supremely badly. He stares down the prospect; beyond the ha-ha cows wade in the grass and further yet an aeroplane rises diagonally from the hedgerows and climbs into the sky, trailing noise. He is worried; it struck him, waking early and restless, that Framleigh might be affecting his inspirational drive. Community living is, of course, essentially healthy and he has been in favour of it for some time now, but he

114

is disturbed by the thought that his identity might be suffering. He examines his identity as he stands there on the Framleigh terrace: it seems to be in good shape but the piece he recorded yesterday lacked a certain . . . well, a certain quality of personal commitment. The strength of the self-analysis was shaky at points. He frowns at the receding Warwickshire landscape, bland in the August sunshine; maybe it is time he looked for a new scene.

By the time Toby and Nick come out onto the terrace Greg has gone. They are trailed by Jason and when, after a further minute or two of conversation, Toby disappears in the direction of the studios, Jason latches onto Nick; he has learned some while since that Nick is pliable, you can usually get him to do what you want. Jason wants his bow and arrows fixed. Paula is too busy to fix them and Toby is too busy to fix them and Greg does not know how to and Bob is not to be found. It is a question of clipping notches in the arrows with a knife and adjusting the string to the bow. Nick sits down on the parapet and gets to work. He says, "What are you going to do with them?"

"Kill things," replies Jason.

Nick flinches, slightly. "What sort of things?"

"Wolves and bears."

"Ah," says Nick, relieved, "are there lots of wolves and bears?"

Jason reflects. "No, there aren't any. So I may kill birds. And rabbits," he adds, remembering the manly line taken by Kevin's dad, with which he was secretly impressed.

Nick says sternly, "That's unkind. They haven't done anything to you."

115

Jason thinks suddenly of blood, which makes him feel funny, but he cannot let on about that, so he is silent for a moment, apparently considering the point. "But they might. If they were big birds. Stab me with their beaks. Or big rabbits might bite."

Nick slots the string into the notch of an arrow, and picks up a different one. "But it wouldn't be fair to shoot them if they weren't actually doing it."

"They might be just going to," says Jason, "without telling me."

Nick hesitates. "If it was another boy you wouldn't start having a fight with him just because he might have a fight with you."

"Not if he was bigger," agrees Jason.

Nick swallows. "Grown-up people . . ." he begins. And then there come to mind various things, such as the photographs in the gun-room of – of Jason's grandfather, as it happens. And other difficulties. "When people are grown-up," he says, "they usually try not to kill animals unless they've got to. To eat them. Just the same as they try not to hurt other people."

"Like not murdering them?" offers Jason.

"That's right," says Nick warmly.

"Then why do they shout at each other and make each other cry?" asks Jason. "And call each other rude names and stick knives in each other and drive cars over each other and blow up each other?"

There is a silence. "Most people," says Nick eventually, "don't." After a further moment he adds, "Lots of people".

Jason, now, is testing the bow-string, which Nick has tightened. "That's tons better. Actually I'm not going to kill anything really. I'm going to make targets on the trees and shoot at them."

"Good," says Nick. "Say thank you," he adds. Nick has been differently raised.

Jason looks at him in surprise. "Thank you. Why do I have to say thank you?" he continues. Wanting, evidently, to know.

"You don't have to," says Nick. "It's just that it's nicer when people do."

"Even if they don't specially want to?"

"Particularly," says Nick, "if they don't specially want to." He looks up at the west front of Framleigh, inscrutable and precariously elegant. From within comes Paula's voice, shouting about something; Toby crosses the Common Room and goes into the hall. "Because the other person might like it. You ought to think about what other people feel like, not just what you feel like." He slams an arrow into the string, raises the bow and shoots a clump of erigeron.

Toby tours the place, making a few unobtrusive adjustments. If he is agitated, this does not show; he moves unhurriedly and stops for a word here and there. He hopes that Mary Chambers feels she is getting something out of the course, and comments warmly on her sketches; he pats Sue on the arm and suggests she has a go at some lino-cutting today. In the gun-room, he removes the notice about phone call charges to guests; he takes, from a cupboard, a selection of family photographs including one of his mother as a debutante in court dress, with tiara, and sticks them up on the mantelpiece. In the former breakfast-room in the east wing, now used as his study, he sweeps from the desk a heap of bills and other papers, some of them menacingly spattered with red type, and stuffs them into a drawer. He gets out a decanter of sherry and some glasses and arranges them on the desk. After some further rummaging around he comes up with an engraved silver salver which he polishes up vigorously on the cushion from the desk chair. Then he goes out through the garden door at the side of the house and crosses the stable-yard to his studio, where he shuffles quickly through a pile of his lithographs and spreads them out on such surfaces as are not already occupied. He glances into Paula's studio and then into the barn, where Bob is mixing clay. He has a word or two with Bob about the extent to which future courses are booked and then goes out once more into the stable-yard, where butterflies are sipping the camomile flowers. Here, Toby pauses: he has spotted a red admiral among the tortoiseshells and peacocks.

Toby's interest in and knowledge of nature is a legacy of his boyhood; like Jason, he roamed the place, observed and, in the fullness of time, put names to things. Rather curiously, though, Framleigh and its surroundings have never featured in his painting; during the fifties and sixties he spent as much time as he could in such places as Greece, Tunisia, Spain and southern France. The flora and fauna that feature in his pictures are the flora and fauna of such places; similarly the landscapes. The shores of the Mediterranean were littered, then, with Toby's friends and colleagues; the light and the inspiration were so much better abroad. Also, it was cheaper. More recently, though, funny things have been happening: the Sunday newspapers run travel articles on places like Wales and the Cotswolds and the Yorkshire Dales. Quite a few of Toby's friends and colleagues have come back and settled in East Anglia or Herefordshire or Barnes or Greenwich. And suddenly it is interesting to know about plants and trees – English ones, too – and admirable to be concerned about the environment. Toby, who is not so much

118

observant as osmotic, has responded to this with alacrity; he has brought out and made public that knowledge acquired in his schooldays, done a suite of lithographs called "Warwickshire Seasons" and tried – unsuccessfully – to put his own immediate bit of the environment to good use. It is not altogether his fault that the Framleigh Field Centre foundered.

Toby is one of those fortunate people who are in accord with their times; he is moving very comfortably through the decade, they suit one another. The same could be said of various of his ancestors: Fox's crony in the late eighteenth century, and the Standish responsible for that section of the former Great Western Railway that now slices through part of the Framleigh estate. Opportunism is of course a quality that the English landed gentry has always had in good measure; such opportunism, though, has usually had a certain chronological motivation: self-interest has been allied with tribal interest, the idea is for things to go on and get better still. Toby's opportunism is different in that it ends with Toby; Jason, who might be supposed to be involved – chronologically – is not, so far as Toby is concerned. He will see that Jason is all right, of course, but he assumes that Jason when mature will wish to do his own thing, just as Toby is doing his own thing.

The butterfly, similarly engaged, moves to a different clump of camomile. Toby looks round the stable-yard; there is nothing further that he can do, indeed his efforts so far seem, as he is well aware, puny. Age and decay are not to be veiled; on the other hand, they have certain acknowledged values.

Chapter Nine

John Lowther, a director of Harpers Bank, pulls into a layby and consults the map. He is heading south from Birmingham, where he had a couple of business meetings, and reckons he must be somewhere near Framleigh by now. Ah yes – there it is, discreetly marked off to the right, only a couple of miles on. He takes his jacket from the hook behind his head, puts it on, glances quickly at himself in the driving mirror, and swings the Rover out onto the road again. A cassette is playing Bach harpsichord arrangements; beyond the tinted windows Warwickshire rolls greenly past – lovely bit of the world, relatively unspoiled round here. Lowther is in a state of comfortable accord with life; his Birmingham engagements went well, now he looks forward to going over this possible site for the Bank's new employee training centre. Fine old house, by all accounts. Run as some kind of art school; amusing people, no doubt.

A few minutes later he turns into the Framleigh drive

(passing, incidentally, Jason and Kevin who are up to nefarious business of their own in a ditch beside the road). Appreciatively, he drives through the park which makes him think vaguely of the National Gallery: all those drooping trees and cows in groups and lavish blue distances. Very pleasant. He rounds the bend in the avenue and sees the house, which impresses in other ways. It suggests such things as good taste and continuity and stability and (oddly enough) prosperity. Lowther's own house, which was built in nineteen sixty-seven is, as it happens, in flattering descent from Framleigh: it too (five-bedroomed detached with two bathrooms, double garage and landscaped garden in exclusive Executive Development) has pillared porch and facade with symmetrical sashed windows; there, though, the similarity ends. Nevertheless, Lowther feels, seeing Framleigh, subtly reassured: the world is orderly, certain things are solid and desirable, he personally is able to recognize which things.

Swinging the car round the gravelled semi-circle in front of the steps, though, on thin weed-infested gravel which does not have the prosperous scrunch that gravel ought to have, he sees that much is awry here, and tuts sadly. One would very much like to be instrumental in giving a helping hand to a place like this; he feels, now, benevolent and influential. Admittedly, Jacobson and other members of the Board seem to have grave doubts about its potential and apparently the asking price at the moment is unrealistic. Well, one will have to take a shrewd look, and form one's own opinion.

It is, now, mid-morning. The various studios are in session. Nick, though, who is hanging around as instructed, sees Lowther's car through the open front door, realizes that the man Toby is expecting has arrived – a little early – and goes quickly over to the stable-yard to alert Toby. Nick is rather vague, as Toby was, about who the man is: a person from a Ministry or something who may be able to help Framleigh financially in some unspecified way. Nick is aware that Toby has the most awful hassles about money and is doing miracles keeping Framleigh going at all.

Nick helps Jean Simpson with a paint problem and then follows Toby back to the house, where he finds him in the process of greeting the visitor. In fact, Toby and John Lowther have just realized, simultaneously, that they were at school together; both have decided to pretend to be unaware of this. They were nine years old at the time; absence of recall would be perfectly understandable. Both, though, have stored the observation as of potential use or interest. John Lowther remembers that Toby was once sick in chapel, had a reputation for unreliability, and always came bottom in maths. Toby remembers that Lowther was fat, sucked up to the masters, had a mother who wore the wrong sort of clothes at Sports Days. Blandly smiling, they shake hands. "You found your way all right?" asks Toby. "What about some coffee?" "Love some," says Lowther. "Bit of a tangle at Redditch, but otherwise no problem. Glorious weather . . ." Nick is despatched to make coffee; the two men move onto the terrace where John Lowther is, as intended, silenced by the prospect, the billowing acreage of trees, the impervious greedy spread of Framleigh's surroundings. "Ah," he says at last, "the famous garden." The final word does not sound appropriate, at all.

Toby learned long ago – as a child, perhaps – that it is seldom necessary to lie. Truth is so easily concealed in other ways.

When there are things you would prefer other people not to know, you simply evade discussion of the things: what is omitted is rarely missed. People notice what is said, not what is left out. Accordingly, he has simply murmured a word or two about Lowther's visit to Paula, Greg, Nick and Bob without further elaboration; they will elaborate for themselves, inaccurately no doubt.

"A man about what?" said Paula, but by that time Toby was halfway out of the room and in any case she wasn't all that interested. Now, seeing Toby approach across the stable yard with a man in a dark suit, a dapper well-shaven man from an alien world, the world she prefers not to inhabit and indeed roundly despises, she sighs theatrically, remarks to her class that they are about to be inspected and to pay no attention, and prepares to receive the visitor.

Lowther sees a fine-looking woman in some sort of long flowing flimsy garment, rather becoming actually. She is surrounded by people fiddling around with bits of mirror and beads and putty. He smiles indulgently. Paula says, hello, do come and look round, hey – mind yourself on that chicken wire . . . She also smiles, and lays a restraining hand on the expensively-suited arm. It has suddenly occurred to her that Toby said something not long ago about a bloke from the Arts Council who might cough up a grant of some kind. Paula is not too clear exactly what the Arts Council is or does except what is evident from its title: it is in her line of business. And it apparently has money, which is something Paula cannot waste time bothering about but – tiresomely – is always needing. So it might be a good idea to be nice.

And, since the things that people say to one another are more often allusive than explanatory, there is no problem. Lowther, who does not want to appear a philistine ignoramus, tours the studio making noises of appreciation. He loves Paula's "Harlequin". "Oh, *do* you?" says Paula. "Oh good . . . Actually *I'm* rather pleased with that. Everyone says I'm onto something there." Lowther remarks upon what a marvellous place Framleigh must be to work in, such a tremendous atmosphere, so evocative . . . "Well, yes," says Paula guardedly; she does not wish to appear too firmly associated with Framleigh, that might not be expedient. "My organization," says Lowther, carefully noncommittal, "is taking something of an interest in Framleigh. There is a possibility of an arrangement that might be beneficial all round." Paula, seeing that her guess has been right, nods. "Oh – super . . . I suppose," she adds vaguely, "it's a question of money?" "Naturally," says Lowther, a touch surprised. For him, practically everything is.

Toby, at this point, intervenes. It might be as well if this conversation did not go too far. He murmurs that there is an awful lot to see yet, and prises Lowther gently from the studio. He takes him over to the pottery, which is in a creative hum; Lowther is amused by Bob and almost tempted to have a go himself. He is impressed by some of Bob's more austere pieces and wouldn't mind buying one, but does not know how to ask the price; this is not, after all, a tradesman exactly. Also, he has no idea what the price might be or how one would know if it was reasonable or not.

Bob assesses the visitor from behind a smokescreen of beard and geniality; he makes, un-noticed, one or two conversational probes.

From the pottery, Toby and Lowther proceed back round to the terrace and thence down onto the prospect. Toby, now, is giving Lowther a curtailed version of the chat to course members on the Framleigh Ideal; there are a few subtle amendments, in view of the audience. What we are trying to do, he says, is make Framleigh something of a retreat, and I mean that in more than one sense. Are you by any chance a Catholic? No, neither am I, but I do feel they have so very much the right idea in the retreat concept . . . Framleigh is a *creative* retreat, both for artists and for ordinary people. And what I envisage, given the financial wherewithal – Toby sighs – is both physical and, how shall I put it, spiritual expansion. I want to get Framleigh into other areas of expression – theatre, film. Put up a complex of workshops, convert the west wing into sleeping accommodation. And I can't help seeing a partnership between Framleigh and your organization as potentially rewarding in so many different ways. Art has always needed patrons. Patrons – he gives a little laugh – have always needed something to patronize. We have a lot to give each other, and it's so nicely symbolic, don't you think?

"Symbolic?" says Lowther, with a slight frown. They have reached the beginning of the woodland rise; they walk through shafts of sunlight in which hang skeins of dust; blackbirds dash shrieking into the undergrowth.

"Your world," says Toby. "The real, day to day world, and the sort of thing we're trying to do. Which are of course," he smoothly continues, "interdependent in every sense. The one sustains the other."

Lowther continues to frown. There are one or two things here he does not altogether care for. That reference to ordinary people did not escape him, and induced a small swell of resentment. I remember you throwing up all over the chapel floor, he thinks, you were fairly ordinary yourself once upon a time. And this talk about partnership isn't quite what's usually implied; the

125

potential rewards look to him to be moving rather firmly in one direction. However . . .

However there is no getting away from the fact that the place is awfully impressive. Members of the Board and their families would of course have special facilities; the idea is that the site eventually chosen – Framleigh or elsewhere – should offer shooting weekends to directors. At this moment, dead on cue, a pheasant erupts from a ditch and hurtles upwards; Lowther, differently clad and with a gun crooked over his arm, escorts a party of friends and associates, telling them of the restoration of the cascade and the grotto which as it happens he has rather taken upon himself, a bit of a personal obsession . . .

". . . the Framleigh Foundation," says Toby, "with of course prominent acknowledgement of the help we've received from your organization." Lowther returns, with a jump, to present circumstances and remarks that the idea is an interesting one. Both he and Toby recognize that this means little or nothing. Toby goes on to discuss the problems of recovering the original park, which has of course always been his great ambition but . . . He shrugs, and gestures hopelessly at the seething vegetation. Indeed, at this point the ride is so overgrown as to be almost swallowed into the woodland; ivy and bramble lap the trunks of the trees and sprawl into the path, stands of nettle and elder and teazle must be negotiated by the walker. Lowther, gingerly picking a length of briar from his trousers, remarks that even so it is all very delightful and of course there is something to be said for real English natural scenery, specially when one is stuck in town most of the time . . . "Well, possibly," says Toby. "But not of course what Kent had in mind at all, the idea of picturesque landscape is entirely different." Lowther senses that he has been put down; he sees, also, that the briar has snagged his suit in three places.

126

At the grotto, he is again silenced. He glances sideways at Toby in his frayed jeans and cheesecloth shirt open to the navel and thinks that if *he* had grown up amid all this . . . Toby, pointing out features of the view, wonders with a combination of interest and disdain what sort of inflated salary a bloke like this is paid; he wonders also if he is wise to be making quite so much of the Framleigh Foundation stuff. In fact, if all that comes to nothing, Toby has a second contingency plan which does not involve Framleigh itself at all, merely the proceeds of its sale. The Framleigh Foundation, or something very similar, could equally well be sited in Provence, Rhodes, Portugal, Marrakesh or many another place.

"Shakespeare country," says Lowther, staring into Warwick-shire, and Toby sighs, though for which of several possible reasons is not apparent.

They reach the end of the woodland ride and return by way of the serpentine rill and the cascade. From time to time there are scurryings in the undergrowth which they either do not notice or dismiss as manifestations of Framleigh's abundant nature; in fact, they are being stalked by Jason and Kevin, who abandoned their ditch activities some time ago in favour of observing the visitor. Figures like him are not often seen at Framleigh. "Who is he?" asks Kevin. Jason, who does not care to admit ignorance, hesitates; "He's a person from the government. He's the Prime Minister's helper." They are both well able to recognize the trappings of power; they have inspected Lowther's car and peered through its windows at the baroque intricacies of its dashboard.

Half way along the prospect, Toby and Lowther are greeted by the gesticulating figure of Greg on the terrace: Toby is wanted on the phone. He hurries in, leaving Lowther to Greg.

127

He has one or two misgivings about this, but there is no alternative.

Greg is hazy as to who Lowther is; Toby murmured something about a man from some ministry. Environment? God knows there is plenty of that in these parts; no doubt guys have to be sent to give it the once over from time to time. Accordingly, he asks Lowther, politely, if he has enjoyed his tour of the park. Lowther, wiping mud from his shoes, replies that it is of course very fine, not that one hadn't a certain idea of what to expect, naturally one is familiar with Rousham and, and . . . (he breaks off – what the devil is that other place called?) . . . and of course it is heartbreaking to see it in such a state though of course one realizes the appalling difficulties owners like Mr Standish . . . Sure, says Greg, who is getting bored – this is one hell of an uninteresting guy.

Lowther is not particularly interested in Greg, either; he hadn't realized there were Americans like this – all the ones he knows are something important in Wall Street and reassuringly like himself though with certain cultural modifications. He asks Greg, kindly, where he comes from and what he does. The second part of Greg's reply ends, temporarily, the conversation. "Ah," says Lowther; he gazes at the house, eyes narrowed, apparently inspecting architectural detail.

The strong sunlight tactlessly emphasizes the cracks in the stucco, the shredding woodwork of the windows, the inadequacies of the roof. "Cost a hell of a lot of money to fix this place up," says Greg, following, it seems, Lowther's thoughts. Lowther nods regretfully and remarks that that is what is worrying his organization.

"You're short on cash?" enquires Greg. Lowther rejoins somewhat sharply that it is a question of financial expediency, simply. Sure, says Greg, you gotta make a lot of hand-outs, I guess, no good dishing it all out to one place. Not at all, says Lowther, we have a single institution in mind, I don't entirely follow your, er . . . In coming to a decision on this particular purchase, he continues, the cost of restoration is very much an active factor.

Greg, at this point, ceases to take a merely desultory interest in the exchange and becomes alert. "Purchase? You people are going to buy the place?"

"There is a possibility," says Lowther smoothly. "At the moment merely a possibility, no more. Framleigh is under consideration by my organization, let me put it like that. Glorious weather, I must say, for this sort of expedition . . ." He swings round and stands looking down the prospect, his hands behind his back; in the mind's eye, Lucinda and the children appear from the trees, having been for a walk or something, and a girl in a frilly apron is bringing out a tray of drinks (catering arrangements would have to be appropriate, in a place like this, none of your hired out-of-work actors).

Greg, at the same moment, grasps what he has been told and realizes that he is in possession of an interesting piece of information that Toby does not intend him or probably anyone else to have. Toby himself now appears through the french windows and suggests that he and Lowther have a sherry in his study before lunch – ". . . which will be strictly informal, we run what you might call a co-operative system for the courses, people seem to prefer something quite simple and easy-going". The invitation, it is clear, does not include Greg, who remains on the terrace, contemplating, as did Lowther, the prospect. It is not, though, the construction of the view, or the misty distances, or indeed the silver hulk of a departing aircraft that occupy his mind.

The studio sessions, now, are over, and the course members gather in the Common Room. Paula, seeing Greg on the terrace, goes out to join him. She sits on the wall, dabbling her feet in sprays of erigeron. "What are you looking at?" Greg grins. "Some real estate, that's all."

At lunch, Lowther is eyed with surprise by the course members, though segregated from them by the Framleigh faculty, who pen him in at the far end of the table. Paula thinks it might be expedient to continue her policy of being nice; Bob is curious; Greg is observing; Nick has to be near Toby. They eat corned beef hash while Toby talks at length about Framleigh, its history, his history, his intentions and anything else that springs to mind; he is, now, a little apprehensive about Lowther's continuing presence and anxious to avert dangerous holes in the conversation into which unwelcome queries might be dropped.

"In the war, of course, St. Benet's School from London was here and as you've seen still is, in a sense. My father never had the money to get the house restored afterwards."

Lowther, bludgeoned into unwariness by the combination of sherry and hash, says, "Nice spot to spend the war, anyway. Damn sight better than Cornwall, that howling gale all the time." Cursing the lapse, he meets Toby's eyes; each knows that the other knows, and knew. "How odd," says Toby smoothly, "I was at school in Cornwall too. It wasn't by any chance . . ." "Good Lord!" exclaims Lowther, less convincingly, "I've just realized, of course you're . . ." "Well, well," says Paula. "I say *do* tell us what Toby was like as a little boy." Lowther fractionally hesitates and his eyes meet Toby's once more. "Alas, buried in the mists of time, I'm afraid – as it is I can only just put the face to the name." "Let me see now," says Toby, with furrowed brow, "wasn't it you who hit a six in the Fathers' cricket match?"; they look again at one another, in naked recollection. Both feel the other has turned out dismally and predictably.

Lunch over, Toby is swift to detach Lowther from everyone else; there is the tour of the house to be completed and then . . . Lowther, glancing at his watch, makes the noises of a busy man whose time is closely allocated. "Quite, quite," says Toby, "which is why we must leave you . . ." He gives the Framleigh faculty his deprecating smile, and leads Lowther away. Bob says, to no one in particular, "And who's Toby's posh friend, then?" "Oh," says Paula busily, "he's someone from the Arts Council, didn't Toby tell you? Having a look round to see if . . ." The sentence vaguely trails. "To see if what?" asks Greg. "Well," says Paula, "to sort of see about buying things maybe." "You figure he's gonna buy some sculptures?" "Well, he didn't actually say, but he loved the Harlequin."

Greg gets up. The course members have already left the refectory and dispersed into the afternoon. "If that guy buys anything, he's buying the whole place. You didn't know? It seems to have slipped Toby's mind to mention it. Excuse me – I have to make a call."

". . . and then just went off for the rest of the session," says Jean Simpson. "I mean, it's all very well leaving Nick to see to things, he's a nice boy but it's not the same, is it? It distinctly says in the brochure 'personal supervision in every studio'. I've not got on today, there are several things Toby's been helping me over and frankly with him not there I couldn't get on at all." She stares at Sue across the Common Room. "Excuse me, Sue, I didn't quite catch that. What did you say?"

"I just said," says Sue, hot about the face but unrepentant, "you aren't the only person Toby's teaching. Actually if you ask me some people expect more than their fair share."

There is an atmosphere of latent mutiny. Resentments have intensified. But mutiny implies some kind of concerted feeling, and hostilities are directed as liberally at one another as at the Framleigh faculty. "That girl," snaps Jean Simpson to Mary Chambers, "wants telling where she gets off." Even Mary is irritable; she is curiously reminded of her school days. People have taken to reserving seats in the refectory for their particular cronies; the arguments about bathrooms have become progressively less genteel.

Keith sits morosely on his own over a mug of Nescafé. He, too, had an unsatisfactory morning: he tried another drawing of the house which was even less successful than the last – this time, the thing did not so much sag in the middle as refuse to be consistent: windows leapt from one plane to another, doors staggered, the roof threatened to crush the whole edifice. Various people, passing by, offered helpful tips which served only to madden. He finds himself particularly inflamed by criticism from women, which is exasperating to a man who knows himself to be absolutely dispassionate where gender is concerned. He has always had women friends with whom sex does not arise; he does not merely think but knows that men and women have equal capacities; he has on several occasions joined in correspondence on the Women's Page of the *Guardian*. And yet today if another of those interfering bitches makes a comment he might well clout her one. There's a kind of woman who always thinks she can do a thing better herself.

It is hot. In the park, the cows swish their tails in pools of shade. The woodland is comatose; no birds sing. There is a distant remorseless sound of combine harvesters.

"And another thing," says Jean Simpson, "that brochure goes on about the swimming pool."

Toby sees Lowther into his car. They shake hands. "So glad," says Toby, "you were able to make it." "Very good of you to give up so much time," says Lowther. "A most useful and er, informative visit. I shall of course give my Board a full and frank report." He is lapped by the leather of the driving seat; he smiles, winds up the smoky window, starts the engine; Toby smiles, waves, stands for a moment watching the Rover's gleaming departure.

In the gun-room, Greg makes another phone call. He talks to a man he met once at a party in London who is in television. He has been wondering for some time if he should look into the TV scene. People say it pays pretty well and it has occurred to him recently that maybe as a medium of expression it has more going for it than one had thought. The man is not, on the face of it, all that encouraging but that may just be British reticence; Greg talks on, and on.

Bob, in his studio, has closed the door, despite the heat, and bolted it from inside. He draws the hessian curtain and inspects a serious of toby jugs fresh from the kiln, awaiting glazing. He works for a while on the prototype of a thatched cottage honeypot, whistling to himself. After a while, apparently satisfied, he takes the old typewriter from the corner and begins a letter to the buyer from the department store in Birmingham; he frowns, his large fingers swamping the keys; letter-writing is not really in his line.

Nick sits in his room, chewing his lip.

Paula and Toby are alone in the library. Toby stands by the floor to ceiling bookshelves in which so few books prop one another up; he wears his most burdened expression. Paula, apparently, is out of breath; her fine breasts rise and fall beneath her orange shirt. The room has that charged feeling of a room in which a good deal has just been said. Toby opens his mouth to speak and as he does so, and before the speech can come, Paula shoots out an arm, plucks the lamp from the side-table and hurls it at him. She misses, but the bulb explodes interestingly.

Outside on the terrace Jason and Kevin lie on their stomachs in the erigeron and the bindweed and the herb robert, peering in. They have had a good morning's stalking, and seen a thing or two already. One of the ladies on the course picked her nose, and someone else was saying nasty things about people. They watch the lamp fly across the room. Kevin's eyes widen in astonishment; it is just like a play on the telly, but real, which is muddling. He says nervously, "She didn't ought to of done that. That costs money, that does". "Bang!" says Jason. "Bang crash! She'll get another one I 'spect. Anyway nobody ever uses it."

Chapter Ten

"What?" says Karen, down there in Dulwich. "Sorry, the children are making a row . . ."

Keith looks across the gun-room; his eyes meet the sepia eyes of Toby's grandfather, who stands amid feathered carnage in nineteen twenty-five. "Cornwall. Or possibly north Wales."

"Oh," says Karen. There is a pause. "Would there be schools there?"

"Of course there'd be bloody schools," snaps Keith. "The Welsh can read and write, can't they?" The same thought, during the night, has occurred to him, which is why he is snapping.

"Well," says Karen, after a further pause, "it's an idea, I suppose. Is it easy to sell hand-crafted furniture, I mean I'm sure you'd be able to make it beautifully, I just wondered if . . ."

Keith, who has also wondered, and told himself that that is craven, snaps again. "Do you always have to calculate about everything? I thought you might be excited."

Down in Dulwich someone – not Karen – has started to cry. Karen sighs. "I shall have to go. Are you enjoying the week?"

"No," says Keith. "I mean yes of course I am."

It is early evening. Light floods through the stained glass window of the gun-room and lies in rainbow pools on the battered carpet. Keith, severed from Karen with a mixture of relief and angry guilt, remains for a while sitting in the armchair. He is dressed for jungle combat in fawn cotton trousers and jacket with many pockets and tabs; he is thinking about getting hold of a lathe from someone next weekend and about Paula and about never going near the bloody lab again and about Karen and about natural inclinations and the suppression thereof. He suspects that he has always suppressed his, and tends to blame his mother. He recalls an argument when he was sixteen about Art or Subsidiary Maths at which Art was dismissed as frivolous and he recalls also the series of microscopes, calculating sets and chemistry outfits given him for Christmas and birthdays; he has, on this sultry evening in the Framleigh gun-room, a feeling that his life has been programmed, and that he has never had much say in the programming. There floats, above the massive Victorian marble fireplace, like a bubble thought in a cartoon, a picture: the picture is of a sunny room in a farmhouse with views onto expansive hilly unoccupied country. The room is cluttered with the wherewithal of making things and in the middle of it Keith sits, making them; in the background a woman who is an odd but enticing mixture of Karen and Paula is . . . well, is just there. Contemplating this, Keith's face takes on an expression of petulance: the expression of a small boy who considers himself deprived. It is not, in fact, at all a characteristic expression; Karen would be surprised.

"She's definitely on the list," says Jean Simpson. "I looked. You two, me, and Tessa Shaw. So where is she, I'd like to know?"

In the kitchen, the same furry apricot light is falling on a sink filled with potatoes. The potatoes require peeling.

"I daresay we can manage," says one of the others. "I'll do half of the spuds and . . ."

Jean Simpson retorts that that is not the point, the girl has no business sloping off and leaving other people to do the work. She observes that as it is she personally has done more than her fair share. Eventually it is decided that Jean should go and look for Tessa: the rest, infected also now with a sense of grudge, start slowly to deal with the potatoes, to open tins, to loudly clatter saucepans.

Jean tours the house, enquiring for Tessa; she has not been seen. Someone suggests she may be over in the studios. Jean goes out onto the terrace, where Jason and Kevin lie on their stomachs beside the lily-pond, interfering with a water-snail, and thence round to the stable-yard. Toby's studio is empty, and so is Paula's. The door to Bob's barn is closed; Jean glances through the window and sees that in fact Bob is there. And so is Tessa. She is sitting with Bob on the large ramshackle sofa covered with old rugs. Bob's arm is around Tessa and as Jean watches his hand comes down over her shoulder and rummages beneath her T-shirt.

Jean steps back from the window. She is filled with some very

137

odd and disagreeable feelings, connected with the fact that she is old enough to be Tessa's mother, that it is a very long time since anyone did that to her, that she has found Bob rather a nice fellow and the niceness was compounded with the peculiar frisson he gave her whenever he stood close to her to instruct her in wheel technique. The frisson, now, turns into something else: a surging resentment.

She bangs on the door. Bob, after a moment, appears. Jean, trying to seem less breathless than she in fact is, wonders if he has seen Tessa. Bob says funny you should ask, she's right here as it happens, come in love. He opens the door wider. Tessa scowls from the sofa. I suppose, says Jean, her voice coming out shriller than she cares for, you've forgotten you're on the kitchen rota. Off you go, says Bob, duty calls. He pats Tessa lightly as she passes, and looks at Jean as he does so, amiably grinning from within the thicket of his beard; her eyes meet his, his friendly twinkling eyes, and she knows that he knows exactly how she feels, and why. It is as though, for an instant, she were naked. As though those regrettable uncontrollable processes within the head were laid bare to the public gaze. She turns and marches away across the stable-yard, followed, ten paces behind, by Tessa.

They do not speak. Tessa is seething. Words like cow and bitch roll around in her mind; she observes with contempt Jean's too-large behind and her boring clothes; she sticks her tongue out at Jean's back, and feels ever so slightly better.

Jean too seethes; she is telling herself in her own familiar matter-of-fact rational voice that the girl had to be made to pull her weight and in any case it was in her own best interests, the silly little fool, a man like that would be after one thing and one thing only . . . And on another level there simmers a distressing

138

soup of emotions, some of them identifiable and others not or at least not in any terms that Jean can acknowledge.

They arrive back at the kitchen and find that the others have just about finished what has to be done.

Nick, earlier, heard the sound of the exploding light-bulb and, shortly after, heard the library door slam and Paula's sandalled feet slap across the hall and up the stairs. He heard Toby go to his study and that door, too, close. For a while he made approaches to the study, determined advances to the door that, each time, ended in withdrawal. Eventually he went out and sat on the terrace.

Where, now, he is joined by Greg, who says "Hi . . . Seen Paula?"

Nick replies that he thinks she is in her room. After a moment he continues, "Greg . . . what you said before about that man, about his bank maybe buying Framleigh . . . are you sure?"

"Sure I'm sure," says Greg, sitting himself down on the wall. "He told me."

"But Toby hasn't ever . . . well, wouldn't he have said something to us?"

Greg shrugs. He looks at Nick, with, it seems, a moment-ary detached interest. "You're really hung up on Toby, aren't you?"

Nick blinks, goes warm around the face, and stares into the pond. The warmth is due as much to annoyance as embarrass-ment: he has no intention of discussing his feelings with Greg, of all people.

"O.K. – that's your problem. But if you were figuring on staying around Framleigh indefinitely, I'd forget it."

"I wasn't," says Nick defensively, "it's just it seems funny that . . ."

But Greg is off, now, in another direction, an older-man-to-younger didactic discourse, somewhat uncharacteristic. "You're an artist, right? Now I don't know how you see yourself developing, but believe me you're never going to get yourself on the right track as long as you're hung up on personal relationships. When I was your age . . ." – here Greg falters, perturbed by an echo of his father, for God's sake – ". . . well, I had to cut loose before I could see inside my own head. There was this girl – well, that's past history now . . . The point is, I couldn't find myself artistically until I was emotionally free. See?"

"Yes," says Nick automatically, and then corrects himself, "I mean no. I don't feel like that."

"You don't?" says Greg, startled. Nick is seldom or never known to disagree.

"I think I'll be a better artist if I have satisfactory relationships with other people than if I don't."

Greg shakes his head sadly. "Yeah, but what's satisfactory?"

"Well," says Nick, looking not at Greg but down the prospect, at the far end of which Jason and Kevin are jumping off the ha-ha, in turn, "I s'pose a relationship in which people try to please each other and not to upset each other and are both prepared to give things up rather than not have each other." He has never, until this moment, formulated this and the sound of it surprises him. He almost forgets Greg, thinking about this; he watches Jason and Kevin, who are now running in the long grass of the park, small leaping unworried (or so it would seem) figures.

"Sounds like a book," says Greg.

Nick is silent. He is disconcerted by his own statement; it bears heavy implications about the inadequacies of his own life, so far. He tries to think with whom he has come closest to this kind of thing, and can find no one; his mother, he realizes, has always behaved thus, but it has been a somewhat one-sided affair. He sees the conduct of parents, suddenly, in a new light. But are they doing what they do out of instinct which might be called a kind of self-interest, or genuine altruism? He frowns.

"Relating to other people," says Greg, "is just fine. That's what we've all got to do. Sure. But you've got to watch out for not getting sold short in the process . . ." – he hesitates, something about that expression makes him uneasy. It smacks of other worlds – ". . . Your responsibility to yourself has to come first. Right? You'll never make it artistically until you get your priorities sorted out. Now this girl I was talking about just now, the trouble with her was she . . ."

Nick stares down the prospect. He continues to think; he sees the many harmonies of what lies before him and is struck by how effectively what people say and do blights their surroundings. If, of course, the surroundings are as exceptional as Framleigh; under other circumstances the process might be reversed. Which is interesting too.

Greg continues to talk.

"I won," announces Jason. "I jumped three jumps further than yours." He rolls on his back in the long grass below the ha-ha; he screws up his eyes at the luminous incandescent clouds that stream above him. He sees dragons, a snouty face, pillows and sheep and great gleaming fish.

Kevin considers this and replies that it is not fair: Jason, he points out, took running jumps whereas he took standing-still jumps.

141

"You could of," says Jason, "if you'd thought of it. Taken running jumps."

"I did think of it," says Kevin, lying, "but I didn't because it wasn't fair. Let's start again."

Jason, who is out of breath, declines.

"All right," says Kevin sulkily, "I won't play any more."

"Don't then," says Jason. They lie, now, side by side, amid the blonde and green and purple flowering grasses and the meadowsweet. Neither stirs, since both are trying to think of a way out of this impasse without loss of face.

Kevin, who is the most aggrieved, shoots a sideways glance at Jason. "Anyway, I've got a Wild West gun and you haven't."

"Don't want one," says Jason. This is untrue; he has raised the matter, recently, with Paula, who says guns are beastly, even as toys, and he can't have one. "I've got a real penknife," he adds. This, as he knows, is a trump card, Kevin being in the same position as regards penknives.

"Foureyes!" says Kevin violently. This is a local term of abuse.

"Foureyes yourself!" responds Jason.

"I know something I'm not telling you," says Kevin.

"Don't care," says Jason, "anyway I know something too."

Above, in the copper beech, collared doves moan; small pale moths flicker among the grass-stems.

Jason heaves himself over onto his stomach. "We'll start again if I have first go."

Kevin hesitates; relief is compounded with lingering grievance. "O.K." he says at last.

Paula, in her studio, with the door closed, tramps around the littered floor; she fiddles with one of the stuffed tight sculptures,

142

makes some corrections to a drawing. The row with Toby has left her both exhilarated and tetchy. Rows, once in a while or indeed quite often, are rather in her line. Nevertheless this one, even though she had not only the last word but most of the others, was unsatisfactory: Toby is undoubtedly up to something and whatever it is does not look as though it will suit her in any way.

If changes are going to be made, then she would prefer to be in on them, if not to have initiated them. If it is to be the end so far as she and Toby are concerned, then she wants to be the one to do the ending. Men do not leave Paula: Paula leaves them. Admittedly, they have both had other arrangements for a long time now, but so far as the world is concerned they are a couple, of a kind, and Paula has a sense of propriety, however eccentric it might seem to some. Arrangements notwithstanding, she and Toby have enjoyed team status, and it looks suspiciously as though Toby is about to let the side down in a big way.

Toby, even when cornered, was enigmatic about his intentions; he got away, Paula realizes with chagrin. She is none the wiser. He murmured elusively about money problems and basic re-thinking of the Framleigh concept and wouldn't let himself be trapped into a straight answer. If he is going to sell Framleigh, then Paula will have to think out her position. If she has to go, then she needs to consider where, and to whom. On the other hand, if this stuff about the Framleigh Foundation is serious, then she is going to have to see that she is firmly at the centre of an enlarged and improved Framleigh and no two ways about it.

Paula has come to expect, over the years, special treatment. Curiously enough, it was during her first marriage that she first became aware of the deference accorded to art. Her husband, proud of her accomplishments, hung her paintings in his consulting-room and boasted to his friends, whose wives were less attractive and had uninteresting occupations in hospitals or offices. He went to great lengths to build a studio into the loft. Paula realized that she had an aura, and learned to display it to good effect. She began to feel different to other people and, eventually, left. She was trapped, she explained to her husband, she needed space and freedom and . . . and people like her.

Actually, people like her have sometimes turned out awkwardly. They have been inconsiderate and unreasonable, often. Her second alliance was with a sculptor who drank a lot and got her pregnant when she hadn't wanted to be (she had to have an abortion, which was upsetting and uncomfortable). Also, he hogged all the studio space. There were times when she almost felt she had been better off before. She left the sculptor for a villa in Ibiza, shared with several other artists. There, the sunshine and cheap food and wine were marvellous, but frictions and rivalries developed and eventually everyone ran out of money. Paula returned to London, and met Toby.

Paula flings herself into the studio chair. She kicks, petulantly, an ethnic cushion. She thinks resentfully that Toby is a sneaky so-and-so, out for himself. Her thoughts pass to Greg and she contemplates, for a while, the idea of going to America; the only trouble about that is that Greg has never actually suggested it. She feels a gush of resentment towards him, also; he is so self-centred and he is always interrupting one. Only yesterday she was trying to tell him about the problems she has run into with the mirror-work and he kept going on about his wretched film stuff; she works herself up into a lather of indignation, recalling this.

The evening sunshine creeps up Paula's bare brown leg. She

144

looks, sprawled there in the basket-chair, like the artlessly arranged subject of a portrait: a beautiful woman at ease. One never, of course, knows what people in portraits are thinking about.

At supper, conversation is muted. Various people do not wish to speak to one another in any case, but these have been careful to separate themselves. Nevertheless, the refectory table is not so large as to put people out of sight or earshot of those they prefer to avoid; glances are exchanged and pointed remarks are made. Tessa observes to Sue that a certain person is a bossy old cow, just like the woman who used to run her Brownie pack. Paula, sighing noisily, says to Keith that she has never in all her life had the emotional support and understanding she needs.

Fifteen people eat corned beef hash (again) and react to one another. There are two days left, now, of the course and its members have a curious sense of detachment, comparable to being at sea on a raft with one shore out of sight and another only barely visible. All except for one person who has reached a decision about severing relations with her boyfriend, and is immersed in rehearsals of what she will say, and another who has twinges of toothache and is thus distracted from the taxing process of human interaction. Few now remember precisely their initial response to Framleigh which has been overlaid by subsequent feelings and events; the onward rush of life has as usual obliterated or distorted the emotions of last week or month or year so that all that matters are the present ones, and the present ones involve a Framleigh which has become personal. All of those round the refectory table are now affected and hence distanced from their routine lives; they have indeed been taken out of themselves. Mary Chambers alone, looking round at the faces, remembers that this was what a number of people had wished for; she thinks also of Toby's expression of the Framleigh Ideal.

She is sitting next to Nick. Opposite is Jason, who has dirt streaked across his face and hands lurid with grass-stains. Mary observes this but it is Nick who says, "Jason, you should have washed yourself before you came to supper".

Jason gazes at him in surprise. "Why?" he asks, as well he may, since this is not something usually recommended by Nick or indeed anyone else.

"Because," says Nick, "it's nicer for other people."

Jason looks at his hands; there are flecks of cow-pat on one palm. Hand-washing is insisted on, as it happens, in Kevin's house and Jason has cheerfully conformed; he has assumed this to be merely local practice, though, and it had not occurred to him to mix the customs of elsewhere with those of Framleigh. He decides it is all too late now and returns to the corned beef hash. "Do you like clean people better than dirty people?" he asks. "I don't."

"It's not that I like them or don't like them," says Nick, "it's just that it's nicer having supper with people whose hands are clean."

Paula, further down the table, is now attending to the conversation. Whether or not she is offended by the implied criticism of her maternal efficiency is not clear. "God," she says, "you really are the original little bourgeois, aren't you, Nick?"

Nick goes crimson. "If you think so."

Keith, attempting intervention, passes a dish of tinned peas.

"No thanks, quite frankly," says Paula. "Those have been in the store-cupboard since kingdom come, I happen to know."

"What's berjwah?" enquires Jason.

"It's having a three-piece suite and a mortgage and cutting the grass on Saturday afternoon," says Paula with a laugh.

This strikes Keith on the raw; he is both offended and defensive. "Frankly I'd have thought it was an attitude of mind."

"That's what that is," says Paula.

Mary Chambers has always believed, rather strongly, in talking to children rather than over or around them. She says, to Jason, "It means people who live in one way rather than in another way. On the whole people who live in houses and aren't particularly poor".

Jason, flattered by the attention, nods. He scrubs one hand furtively against his jeans.

Paula opens her mouth to comment, and then thinks better of it. There is an unwritten Framleigh rule that one is nice or as nice as possible to course members and even in her present heightened state she is loth to break it. She starts a conversation with Greg, down the table, to indicate boredom.

Nick, who has thought, too late, of various things he could or should have said to Paula, sits in seething silence. Jason, who has now lost interest in the whole business, looks up and down the table and sees mouths opening and shutting, quack-quack like ducks, or like the tadpoles in the pond gobbling at the water-weed, He mimes this, making a popping noise with his lips.

Toby, who is in any case exhausted, has an unpleasant feeling that things are slipping out of control. There have before now been courses that have become somewhat out of hand; there was the time Bob got plastered and had a fight with a chap whose girl he'd been messing about with, and the time a woman

147

from Liverpool had hysterics and the time people got food-poisoning. But this particular course has about it a sense of impending crisis; perfectly ordinary people are beginning to behave as though they were prima donnas. That red-haired woman collared him before dinner, complaining about the domestic arrangements and hinting darkly at something or other; the girl Sue, who was quite amusing to begin with, is getting beyond a joke. And he is getting damn all support from anyone else – Paula in one of her rages, Nick in an odd mood, Greg sloping around looking smug.

Moreover, Toby suspects that the deal with Harpers is either going to be extremely sticky or will fall through altogether.

Just as he has always preferred evasion to lying, Toby has also favoured pacification to confrontation. He looks round the table, at the various faces on which ill-temper is manifest; some kind of conciliatory move, he decides, is necessary. He clears his throat, treats course members and faculty to his most deprecating smile, taps on the table with a fork, and speaks.

Chapter Eleven

"Are you mad?" Paula demands of Toby, in the middle of the prospect.

They are in the middle of the prospect because Paula has hissed, dangerously, that she wants a word or two, and the middle of the prospect is the only place Toby can immediately think of where they will not be overheard. Paula's words, as he knows from experience, are not always all that quiet.

Toby sighs.

"A picnic outing for the kiddies!"

"I am merely," says Toby coldly, "trying to keep people happy. This course is not one hundred per cent successful. People are restive. I am not blaming anyone in particular; I am simply stating a fact. I am simply trying to maintain what I consider to be Framleigh standards."

Paula snorts. "And to keep up Framleigh standards we've all got to go on a bloody afternoon outing!"

"There is no compulsion," says Toby, "on anyone. The Framleigh Ideal, as you well know, has always been for people to do their own thing. I had always thought you and I agreed on that. If you prefer not to come . . ." – he shrugs – ". . . then it's my problem. I shall take the course members on my own."

"They could go without any of us," snaps Paula.

Toby looks down the prospect, over the seething summer grass and into the elegant distances of the park. "I daresay. But I happen to feel a responsibility."

"Oh, I know," says Paula, "you're so much better brought up than I am. It's very classy to have a sense of responsibility."

They glare at each other. Toby says, with the strained patience of one who knows himself to be tried beyond endurance, "That is childish, Paula".

"Huh!" says Paula. "That's rich, from you. Who cheats at liar dice? And gets in a paddy when he loses at croquet?"

"I bloody well don't," Toby retorts.

Paula laughs. Toby turns and starts to walk off. He says, over his shoulder, that Paula can suit herself, so far as he is concerned: if she is no longer interested in Framleigh or the courses then maybe she had better stay behind.

In the event, Paula decides to go because Greg is going and because anyway she can't stand being left on her own. Greg goes because he is feeling restless and he certainly doesn't want to be involved, just now, in a solitary tête-a-tête with Paula. Nick goes because Toby wants him to. Bob goes for the hell of it. The course members go because Toby or Paula or Bob are going or simply because it sounds as though it might be fun. Jason would have liked to go had he known what was afoot, but does not get a chance. He is bundled off to Kevin's house and told to stay there till later.

Toby's scheme of a visit to Warwick Castle followed by an outing on the river at Stratford is designed as a measure of pacification; the course has only one more day to run and something like this, he feels, a gesture of goodwill, might put people in a better frame of mind and salvage things. Toby, curiously, has a protective sensitivity about Framleigh's good name. Also, he is nervous of Greg's mood and Paula's mood and the suspicions aroused by Lowther's visit and wants a diversion of some kind. The landscape, once more, will come in handy.

The minibus, plus one car, will accommodate them all. Greg will drive the minibus and Mary Chambers offers the use of her car. At once, on the weedy gravelled drive, at the foot of the pock-marked Framleigh steps, there is tension. Sue, of course, wants to sit with Toby and Tessa with Bob. Jean Simpson wants to get as far from Tessa as possible and feels herself flushing every time she looks at Bob. People shuffle around, manoeuvring. In the end Sue finds herself beside Nick, with Toby at the other end of the vehicle, and Tessa is forced into the back of Mary's car with Keith, where both travel in silence: Tessa sulking and Keith in furious irritation with himself, with Karen, with Paula, with life and its inadequacies.

Greg drives fast. Too fast. He drives with one elbow propped on the sill of the open window. Toby sits just behind him, at the end of the minibus bench. There is an interesting reversal of status: Greg, now, is top person. The driver of a vehicle is always top person. "Slow down, for Christ's sake," mutters Toby. "You'll have this thing in the ditch." Greg, in response, accelerates to overtake. "Yessir," he says, "right, sir. Anything you say, sir." Further back in the minibus, someone giggles. Greg grins, stretches, slouches back in the driving-seat.

There is chatter, and banter; people say things that are

straightforward and also things that in fact mean quite other things. These are the same people as rode in the same minibus a few days ago. Only up to a point, though – partly because two or three are absent and two or three others present – but more because those present are not precisely the same; they are changed by time and proximity and they are chattering and bantering with people who are similarly changed and towards whom they have feelings and responses, both agreeable and disagreeable. Some people are in love with other people and some people despise other people and some are relatively indifferent and Paula is consumed by a (not unfamiliar) longing to hit Toby on his balding head and Bob is very much in need of a drink and proposing to push off to the nearest pub when they get to Warwick, if by good luck they're still open, it being now going on two o'clock.

When they are all disembarked, in the car park, it becomes clear that unity will be difficult to achieve. Paula announces that she has seen the wretched place anyway and is going to sit on the castle lawns. Bob, glancing at his watch, says he'll join them presently; Tessa watches his departing back and her face sags. Keith thinks maybe he'll pass up the guided tour, too, and hang around outside. In the end it is Toby and Greg who lead away the depleted party, to peruse the Van Dycks and the suits of armour and the triptych segments of the Avon displayed in mullioned frames.

In the pub, Bob chats up the girl behind the bar and manages to extend opening time by five minutes or so. Keith follows Paula onto the castle lawn where to his fury they are joined by Jean Simpson. Jean, also, has seen the castle; she and her husband brought the kids here once. She recalls the occasion, at length; Paula, not bothering to conceal a yawn, moves off a few yards and stretches out on the grass. Keith sits sullenly on a bench with

152

Jean, not responding to her narrative or to any subsequent conversational moves. He wonders if he really likes women as much as he has always thought he did; he tries to think of any men as awful as some of the women he has come across, or as maddening as some of those he has known well. Jean, who is able to talk about one thing while thinking another, eyes his jeans and denim jacket and congratulates herself on being married to someone who still knows how to dress decently for a fellow of forty plus.

Paula, apparently, sleeps.

The castle party emerges. Sue is pink and smiling: plunging, at one point, down a narrow flight of stairs, she found herself next to Toby who placed a solicitous and, she feels sure, meaningful, hand under her elbow. "All right, love?" he asked. The word repeats itself in her head.

Greg is bored and becoming fretful. It bugs him that he cannot think how to exploit his conversation with Lowther. Here he is, in interesting possession of the sure fact that old Toby is planning to sell the place behind everyone's backs, and when he passes this on to the others all they do is whine like a lot of kids. At least, Paula makes it an occasion to have a row with Toby which she would do anyway, and Nick goes into a lot of introspective stuff about relationships. Only Bob there looks like having an adequate sense of self-preservation.

Bob reappears. Genial, now.

They re-embark, after further manoeuvrings on the part of those for whom the success or failure of the whole afternoon depends on desired proximities. Toby, this time, gets into the back of Mary's car and Sue beats Nick to the other door, in an unseemly scurry that has them treading on each other's feet. Toby, from the car, slightly smiles.

Stratford, of course, is awash with people. Paula looks round, through the enormous sunglasses that swamp her face, and sighs theatrically. "Well," she says, to Toby "you brought us here, now what?"

But Toby can trump this. He knows one of the people who hire out boats and has telephoned ahead. There are punts ready and waiting: the right number of punts, lined up at the river bank. "Oh, how gorgeous!" cries Sue. All the women become, for some reason, girlish. Water and boats have an odd effect on people.

There is question, now, of who is to do the punting. Bob has already rolled up his shirt-sleeves. Keith remarks casually that he doesn't mind driving. The third punt, it seems, must fall to either Toby or Greg. The other men – Nick and a television cameraman called Sam – are both unassertive and physically slight. It seems right that the manipulator of a punt-pole should be a dominant figure.

Toby says, "Greg, will you get in with Keith and the girls. I'll take this one."

All, now, are placed; hardly anyone is where they would wish to be, except for Paula, who has established herself in the punt with the most cushions, which happens to be the one managed by Bob. She has made herself as comfortable as possible, and looks strikingly more handsome than anyone else, and also as though she were only fortuitously of the party. Strangers eye her.

It turns out that Toby is very good at punting. Keith and Bob are adequate, but Toby's craft sweeps ahead down the river; he is stylish, and effortless. Sue is in a terrible state, twenty yards behind.

Mary Chambers is in an odd state of mind. Since she is as good at observing herself as she is at observing others, she knows this, and is the more disconcerted. She is having various

154

unfamiliar feelings. For example, she is very aware of Paula: she finds herself wishing she looked like Paula. She has not felt like this about another woman since she was about sixteen and envied her best friend's blonde curls. She feels piqued because Bob has not addressed a word to her all afternoon, and she rather likes Bob. She was jealous of Jean Simpson, this morning, because during Toby's studio session Toby made much of Jean's drawing and hardly glanced at hers, which was manifestly better. Neither envy, pique or jealousy are, in the normal way of things, part of her repertoire. She is perhaps unusual. Fermenting with all this, she sits silent at one end of Keith's punt.

The day is perfect: there is sun and a warm breeze. Chips of light sparkle on the water; the banks are soft with shifting flowing grasses; the air is full of the sound of birds, of the summer wind in the trees. From somewhere there is a smell of mown grass.

Jean Simpson says, "That's better. Now we're away from all those people". Paula, at the other end of the punt, makes a spluttering sound that might be derisive or might be accidental; Jean, alert, looks at her suspiciously and then away at the river. "Gorgeous afternoon," she adds. Jean needs to talk when ill at ease.

They are approaching, now, a point where the river narrows and is swept for two-thirds of its width by low-hanging trees. Toby is forced by an oncoming canoe to pull in towards the trees: tails of willow sweep his head and arms and as he turns sideways to manoeuvre away from the canoe four people see that the harmless leaves conceal also a hefty branch, which if Toby does not quickly duck will . . .

Paula, in the following punt, sees and watches with interest. Greg, also, sees and sits up a little more alertly. Mary Chambers sees, opens her mouth and then for some extraordinary reason closes it again. She sits frozen by her own inaction and by what is about to . . .

Sue sees and shouts, "Toby, look out!"

Toby turns his head and ducks. Too late to prevent the branch swiping him but in time to have it send him sprawling not into the river but on top of the other occupants of the punt. There are cries and protests and some laughter and the punt swings sideways into the bank. "Great stuff!" calls Greg. "Let's have it again."

The punts drift together. Toby gets up, blank-faced. Nick says, "Are you O.K.?"

Toby holds his hand to his back. "I think," he says, "someone else may have to take over for a bit."

Paula lowers her sunglasses and stares over the top of them. "Oh for heaven's sake, you can't have hurt yourself!"

Toby hands the punt-pole to Greg; he wears the martyred expression of a man riding out intense physical discomfort. He sits, stiffly. "Shall we go on?"

After a couple of minutes Toby says, "Greg, you'd do better if you didn't climb up the pole. Lift and drop."

"O.K., O.K.," snaps Greg. Water sprays the occupants of the punt. "Oops!" says Tessa, wiping her arms.

The punt lurches. Greg has all but lost the pole; he grabs, just in time.

"That," says Toby, "is the classic boob. Don't run up and down the punt like that."

Greg slams the pole down into the water. "I guess you have to be born to this kind of thing. Like one or two other features of life around here."

"And what exactly do you mean by that?" asks Toby.

"Oh, cut it out!" says Keith.

Heads turn, in all three punts. "What?" says Toby, startled into genuine enquiry.

"I said cut it out. The both of you."

"Well," says Jean Simpson, to the willows and the sparkling water and the mallard upended by the bank, "temper temper . . ."

Nick is now suffering the curious form of distress induced by the humiliation of a person with whom one is infatuated: a compound of embarrassment and sympathy. Mary Chambers is still contemplating her own response with amazement: she rather wanted, she realizes, to see Toby fall in the river.

The punts proceed downstream. Greg's style does not improve; his punt swings from one side of the river to the other and Toby sits at its end with folded arms, loudly saying nothing. Bob shouts, "Move over!" and takes his party past. At once Keith, behind, speeds up. "Hey!" cries Sue. "You're soaking me! This isn't a race." Paula trails her hand in the water; she looks down the river at Keith and, he is sure, smiles conspiratorially. Unless, of course, it is a trick of the light. He is exasperated, suddenly, by the way Bob is hogging the river, ahead. He points out that the rules of the road apply on water just as much as on land and suggests that Bob keep left. Bob, grinning, flicks water with the end of his punt-pole. The spray misses Keith and catches Jean Simpson, who dries herself ostentatiously. "Actually," she says, "I don't call that funny."

Presently the river widens. Keith, with an effort that has him copiously sweating, puts on a spurt and overtakes Bob. "My," says Paula, as the punt passes, "that's very manly stuff, Keith". Bob, now, is scowling. Tessa, now alongside, tries vainly to catch his eye; he is avoiding her, she knows he is, something has happened, it is all over, she knows it is . . .

157

Keith, methodically raising and dropping the pole, feels terrific. Calm and controlled and terrific.

They are approaching another punt party composed of French schoolchildren. Blasts of transistor radio and strident voices rake the willows and the sunlit grassy banks. Jean Simpson, staring, remarks that if there are any teachers with that lot they aren't, frankly, doing much about controlling them. Paula winces at the transistors, putting her hands over her ears. "Barbarians," she says, without bothering to lower her voice. The young French pass comments on the Framleigh party which are perfectly understood by several of them. "One does, as it happens," says Paula loudly, "speak French." At this point a girl pushes a boy into the river and any further comment is swamped by shrieks and laughter. The thrashing punts are left behind.

"It's people like that," says Jean Simpson, with a sigh, "who ruin places like this."

The punters, now, are beginning to flag. It is Greg who gives in first and proposes a stop. A length of bank ahead offers a place for all three punts. Toby, in a weary voice, gives instructions about tying up securely. "And stick the pole in alongside," he tells Greg, "that's what one does."

"Does one?" replies Greg. "Just fancy . . ." Toby gets from the punt with exaggerated care, one hand to his back. Others alight also. Paula stands pointedly until Keith comes forward to offer assistance. She remarks that there is something to be said for old-fashioned good manners. Keith smirks. Greg, though, has not heard. He has flung himself down on the grass in the sun.

They are in a meadow – a buttercup meadow, gold-splashed from one end to the other. There are great swathes of meadow-sweet, too, and a blue veiling of vetch on the river bank and here and there a soldiery of clover heads. Warblers singing from the

158

reeds. A pale blue sky marbled with thin high clouds. Sun. Water.

No one, though, pays much if any attention to all this. All are concerned with feelings and with the effect they are having on others or the effect those others are having on them. Mary Chambers tingles with irritation and hostility towards almost everyone. She has not felt like this for a long time; for so long, indeed, that she cannot at first place the distant echo of the emotion. Then it comes to her: the jungle reactions of the Upper Fourth, time out of mind ago at Worcester High School for Girls. It is as though some disease of the personality, long tamed, were to spring once again to energetic life. She steps from the punt to the bank, and finds a patch of grass on which to sit. Others dump themselves around her: Jean Simpson and Nick and Sue and Bob and Tessa. Paula and Keith. Toby props himself against a tree. When asked by Nick how his back feels, he says he is all right, thanks, his tone implying the opposite.

"You want to watch it," says Jean, "with back things. My husband was laid up three weeks the year before last."

Paula sits amid buttercups. She is wearing a long dress patterned in reds and mauves, a string of amber beads; her hair is loose and wild, with a silk scarf somehow threaded amongst it but not holding it together. She looks pre-Raphaelite; she also makes all the other women feel drab. She says, "I used to have the most ghastly trouble with my back once. I couldn't paint for weeks."

"Yes, Paula," says Toby wearily, "I remember." Paula does not hear. She continues, "I still have to be careful not to lift heavy things."

"George was off work a month," says Jean Simpson.

Both Toby and Paula have placed themselves a little apart from everyone else. Some people have gone for a stroll along the

159

bank. Bob and Tessa have disappeared, unregarded by the rest (which is odd, as Tessa's uprush of emotion should surely be as potent as the smells and sounds of the place).

Mary Chambers observes Toby, and Paula. The way in which they are sitting slightly apart does not escape her; she realizes, though, that she no longer feels, as she did five days ago, that they, or Greg, or Bob – or indeed Nick, but Nick was always a subordinate, as it were – are persons of a different order. And furthermore they are both, today, annoying her. As indeed is almost everyone. She dismembers flower-heads, and listens despite herself to what others are saying.

Paula and Jean are still talking, independently, of Paula's and of Jean's husband's back ailments. Sue is asking Toby what those reeds are called, over there, and Toby is replying in a detached and impersonal way that has Sue looking suddenly glum. Nick is just sitting.

Thinking, in fact, that he would like to be alone. Alone and uncaring like. . . like the reeds and the monotonously singing bird somewhere within them and the cow wading through the meadowsweet.

"Of course," says Paula, "it's not really the same thing at all . . ." The sentence trails. She is dissociating herself, as everyone at once realizes, from Jean's husband.

Mary Chambers looks up. "Why?"

Paula turns and stares at her; course members do not normally query her thus; Mary is not the sort of person who thus queries.

There is a silence, into which Sue rushes to say that well after all it's different, isn't it? I mean, doing a job isn't the same as being an artist. She glances quickly at Toby; the remark, in so far as it is contrived at all, is intended to please him while also giving offence to Jean Simpson.

"It's a question of commitment, isn't it?" says Toby with a smile. It is not clear if he is subtly closing ranks with Paula or putting down Mary.

Jean, offended, remarks that as it happens George is very dedicated to his work and that in point of fact he'll be senior manager next year.

Mary looks at them all. She doesn't much like any of them, she realizes. She wishes she could clap her hands and make them disappear. Or cry, "You're nothing but a pack of cards!" Nick she might allow to remain, along with the sunlight on the river and the bird in the reeds and the distant, decorative cows. She feels distinctly aggressive, a most unfamiliar response.

"If I'm not working," states Paula, "I'm simply not myself, that's all there is to it."

"People," Mary snaps, "aren't what they are because of what they do."

Paula gazes at her in astonishment, and distaste. "Well, really . . ." she begins.

Greg interrupts. "That doesn't make sense."

"What doesn't?" says Mary, dangerously. She knows, all of a sudden, that she is not going to be told what does or doesn't make sense by Greg, of all people.

"It's a question of what you mean," says Greg, lying on his back, hands clasped behind his head. "Of what you mean by 'are' and 'do'. Words are tools. Meaning is what you dig for. I assume that what Paula means, and what you mean, is that . . ."

"Oh, be quiet!" exclaims Mary.

Everyone, now, stares at her. It is as though she were manifesting visible and startling symptoms of disease: smallpox, leprosy. Paula is quite genuinely surprised to be confronted with a display of temperament in one who is just an ordinary person.

She wonders if perhaps the woman is ill. Toby's expression is one of absolute weariness, as though tried beyond endurance by the vagaries of others.

"The way you go on . . ." says Mary. "Some of you . . . sometimes . . . It's enough to put people off what you're doing and actually what you're doing is important. I don't mean what you personally are doing but the thing . . . creating, if only there was some other word for it because that one doesn't much mean anything any more . . . it's probably more important than anything but when it gets mixed up with thinking that what you do makes you what you are then . . ." She stops, swallows, her face is a dull red and her eyes slightly bulge. She says, "I'm sorry but that's how it seems to me".

They gaze, variously reacting. Paula, who particularly disliked the bit about what you personally are doing, sorts out several replies with rather more deliberation than is usual for her. Toby closes his eyes. Jean Simpson says, "Well, I must say I think that's a bit strong. Personally . . ."

Keith is standing up. It seems at first as though this too is some kind of response to what has been said but he is in fact looking not at Mary but towards the river. "Oh Christ, one of the damn punts has gone."

They all, now, look.

"And I left my bag in it!" cries Jean. "With twenty-eight pounds and my cheque book and the Barclaycard . . . "

Greg is saying that he put the darned pole in and anyway I thought *you* were tying it up, Toby . . . and Paula is saying that yes, you should have checked, after all this whole thing was your idea . . . and Toby breaks in to say that it wasn't his idea frankly to crack his spine and Greg as it happens was doing the punting so it was up to him to see the thing was tied up properly.

162

". . . and all those wretched French kids are just along there!" wails Jean at which Greg exclaims fairly but not quite sufficiently inaudibly that of all chauvinist remarks that just about . . . and Paula is telling Toby, who is on his feet staring down the river, that there doesn't seem much wrong with his back now . . . and Greg has gone on to point out that in fact Keith's punt is drifting downstream and very likely dislodged the other one and . . .

Into which exchange of opinion Nick breaks to shout that all this is pointless and what they have to do is get the punt back, using one of the other punts.

"Why was Greg all wet?"

"Because he fell in the river."

"Why did he?"

"Because," says Paula, "the punt was stuck in the mud and people were silly about getting it unstuck."

"Was Toby silly?" asks Jason with interest.

"Yes," says Paula, "I mean no."

"Was Greg silly?"

"Yes," says Paula crisply.

"Why was the lady cross?"

"Because her dress got dirty."

"Did someone push her?"

"Of course not," snaps Paula, "it was an accident."

"It's not fair," says Jason, aggrieved, "why couldn't I come out in a boat too?"

"Because," says Paula, "it wasn't for children. It was a grown-up time."

Chapter Twelve

Framleigh, on this last morning of the course, is washed with sunshine. Sun has the early mist smoking up from the prospect and a haze of midges spinning above the lily-pond. It flashes from the wire angles of "Introspective Woman" and falls across the bed in which Paula lies with Greg. Greg is outlining some thoughts he has had about a poem sequence and Paula is thinking about clothes: she knows suddenly that she cannot go for much longer without a dark blue cheesecloth dress, full length, with some kind of braiding effect around the sleeves and hem. The events of yesterday, for both, have shrivelled to insignificance; both have experienced that kind of occasion often enough before and in any case both are people conveniently able to shed tiresome or inconvenient pieces of the past. Paula forgets about boring things, and Greg translates personal humiliations into more advantageous events. That damn fool punting business, for instance, he now realizes, could be used symbolically: the river of life or something like that, and the poet's creative strivings against the hostile currents of . . . of . . .

Mary Chambers stands naked in front of the mirror. She ignores the person pointedly shuffling outside the door because she also has done plenty of waiting for the bathroom and it is her turn now. She appraises herself: she is not as handsome as Paula or as young as Sue and Tessa but she is not bad, all the same. It is a long time since she looked at herself thus. She decides that when she gets home she will throw away most of her clothes and get new ones. In order to pay for these she will put in for a salary rise which as it happens is long overdue anyway: she is worth, she reckons, about a third as much again as she is getting. She will point this out, quietly but firmly. She will also tell her husband that she would like to spend the money set aside for a greenhouse on painting equipment; they can do without a greenhouse. And she will have her hair cut differently and tell her mother-in-law that no, she cannot come to stay for three weeks in September.

Nick says, "Toby, there's something I've been rather wanting to ask you about . . ."

Toby dresses: not a lengthy process. "I've got some phoning to do. Later – O.K.?"

"It's about whether if I go on, well, being here, I could run a design studio for the courses . . . I thought maybe . . ."

Toby sighs. "If only one could do everything one would like to do."

". . . if we turned the billiard room into another studio . . ."

Toby makes a despairing gesture. "Cash?"

Nick swallows. "But I thought . . . well, this bank . . . if you're going to . . ."

"Going to what?" says Toby coldly. "I've got a thousand things to do this morning, Nick. You really must not *nag*."

Keith stamps up and down outside the bathroom door. When eventually Mary Chambers emerges they barely greet one another. She has splashed water all over the floor, he notes: women always do that. He shaves, and thinks of yesterday, with faint disbelief. He remembers how he felt suddenly exasperated with the whole damn lot of them (with one or two exceptions, maybe); he remembers, in astonishment, telling Toby and Greg to shut up; he remembers, and the morning is enhanced by the memory, Greg trying to shove the punt out of the muddy bank and shoving too hard and losing his balance. He remembers Paula in that long flowery dress, dappled with sunlight, talking. When, though, he tries to remember what she was talking about he finds that it has dissolved into an unmemorable flow; she sounds once again worryingly and of course quite inaccurately like his mother. Or Karen's mother. Or Karen, occasionally.

Jason is making himself a den in the undergrowth beside the prospect. He may let Kevin share it with him; they may make a fire and catch rabbits and cook them and live here all the time; he may cut down big trees and saw the branches off and make a better den like a real little house. He wanders, picking up sticks.

He finds a splinter in his finger and chews at it. He looks towards Framleigh and sees people on the terrace and remembers that he has not had any breakfast.

Toby comes through the french windows. He glances around. "All here? Great. I'll sort out studios in a moment but first there's just one or two things I'd like to say."

He pauses. Jean Simpson, who is sitting on the terrace wall telling people about this weekend cookery course in Devon she has heard about, stops talking. So do others. They look towards Toby, just as they did five nights ago. The looks, though, are tempered now by experience: some people are more interested, and others less so. Toby is a known quantity, for better and for worse; and he, for his part, sees faces that are not strange but invested with his own responses. Not, on the whole, that course members evoke much of a response from him: they are not really his kind, when all's said and done.

"Well – last day! I know we've had one or two irritating hang-ups on this course, but you've all been marvellous about mucking in and I hope you feel as I do that in the end what matters is the Framleigh atmosphere and the work you've been doing. For my part . . ." – he looks round with a quick, deprecating smile – ". . . for my own part I always feel at the end of each course that I've learned a lot myself. Creativity is a matter of give and take, isn't it? I want you to have felt that you've had a chance to see what it's all about. And that you've been able to step aside from the rat-race and learn a bit about yourselves too. That's what living with other people does, right? There – enough of that! More work now – do what you like this afternoon – and tonight we have our farewell party. Eight onwards. Now – who wants to be where this morning?"

Everyone is allocated. Tessa, returning to her room to fetch a Kleenex, comes through the empty house and hears the phone ringing in the gun-room. "Hello?" she says. A man's voice indistinctly replies, far down windy tunnels: he seems to ask if she is Mr Standish's secretary. "No," says Tessa, her mind on Bob: he said, last night, he casually said, that he might be up her way next month. She has been in a turmoil ever since; she hardly slept a wink. The voice crackles on about someone called Butters and negotiations and the possibility of a discussion tonight. Yes, she says, I'll tell him. She puts the phone down and hurries back to the stables. What would Mum say, confronted with Bob? She tries to picture him at home, at her home, and fails. Did he mean it? Could he have meant it?

In the studios, this morning, there is considerable application. People want to finish what they have been doing and have some demonstrable achievement to take away with them. Those who have successfully potted are the most satisfied: there are ashtrays and mugs and bowls. Jean Simpson has a bead and mirror sculpture about which, privately, she has doubts: she just cannot see it in the living-room at home and may in fact quietly dispose of it on the way back. But it would not do to say so. Mary Chambers has several pleasing pictures. Sue has two drawings with which she is secretly rather thrilled. Keith has nothing; somehow no single endeavour was completed. In view of this he decides to spend the morning in Bob's barn; it is too late to equip himself even with an ashtray but he may as well have another look at what goes on there. Come to think of it, pottery might be an idea. He is still a mite uneasy about the craft furniture scene. Once in the barn, though, he is chagrined to see that even the most banal and apparently untalented people have turned out perfectly agreeable, even aesthetic, objects. This is food for thought. He hangs around the studio after the others have gone, looking at things. Bob's stuff, ranged around on shelves, is of course in another class altogether, that one can see . . . Keith picks up Sam's bowls and Tessa's mug, frowning slightly. He wanders to the end of the room and peeks behind a hessian curtain. What he sees there stops him dead. Jesus Christ! He gazes, in blank astonishment and then with dawning comprehension at the ranks of toby jugs and thatched cottage honeypots. Well, well, well . . .

Greg, in a fit of goodwill, has volunteered to take care of the mid-day meal. He sets the refectory table and opens a lot of tins and unwraps several loaves of bread and a few packets of margarine and as he does so it occurs to him that it will be a hassle if things go on like this. No one, so far as he knows, has done anything about replacing the Filipino girls. However that is not his headache since his plans for the immediate future, let alone any other kind of future, are fluid. He might take off at any moment. Or on the other hand he might not. Greg believes in personal adaptibility. You want to be flexible in your approach to life, if you're going to live creatively: flexible in outlook, flexible in relationships. He fills jugs with water, and puts them on the table – which reminds him that if these guys are going to be given any kind of a send-off tonight someone had better get in some drink, which means the usual whip-round: Toby does not include this kind of thing in the Framleigh budget. Today's goodwill, Greg benignly decides, will take him so far as seeing to the whip-round and running the minibus to the off-licence in Woodbury.

"I gave two pounds," says Jean Simpson. "I mean, frankly, that's more than enough – it's not as though I'm going to get through a whole bottle of wine personally. But you have to show willing."

There is an atmosphere, that afternoon, of unfinished business. People do not seem able to settle to anything. Some return to the studios, and then drift out again. Others walk in the park, but there is something melancholy and lowering about the day, despite the sun: the trees stand heavily in the landscape, nothing moves, the place is stuck in the endless lethargic present of an English August afternoon. Those who have wandered off down the woodland ride, or in search of the cascade and the temple, change their minds and come back: they feel oppressed by all that torpid greenery. "It's a funny thing about the country," says Jean, "but it's when you're not in it that you most want it, if you see what I mean. When you are it can seem a bit pointless."

Even Jason is infected. Kevin has gone out for the day to see his grandmother. Jason says to Paula, accusingly, "I've got no one to play with".

"Play with the tadpoles in the pond."

"That's no good," Jason snarls, "they don't play back, do they?"

"Play in your den," says Paula, heading off upstairs.

"How can I play with myself?" bawls Jason. But Paula has business of her own; besides, she has always maintained that children are no problem so long as you don't let them run your life. Jason, who vaguely knows his mum is not like other people's mums, and also vaguely sees advantages in this (penknives, agreed mutual non interference . . .) drifts back outside, to the old kitchen garden, where he spends a while hitting the wall with various sticks, until they break.

Greg inspects bins stuffed with bottles, raucously priced, and picks out some Spanish and some Algerian and some nice cheap stuff that has no label. "These don't have a label," he says to the guy behind the cash-register, who indicates a wire tray: "You want a label? Plenty of labels in there." Greg, intrigued, forages and selects Chateau Something 1969. The guy slaps the labels on the bottles and the bottles into a box, wrong end up in some cases so as to get them all in.

The afternoon seeps away. It seeps into an evening that is cooler and brisker and in which people begin to feel more vigorous and perhaps more charitably disposed to one another. Tessa gets out her long, white pin-tucked and sashed and frilled Laura Ashley dress that she has been saving up for tonight. Sue washes her hair. Keith has a restorative whisky from his emergency kit because he is feeling edgy; he does not feel much less edgy afterwards but an element of aggression is added, which might be interesting. Mary Chambers phones her husband to say that she will be home by lunch-time tomorrow. When her husband mentions – in passing and without rancour – that there does not seem to be anything much in the fridge for supper tonight she refers him quite tartly to the local fish and chip shop. Those on kitchen duty get a meal together, rather more enthusiastically than of late. Greg decides to make a wine cup. He sends Nick out into the garden to gather herbs and searches the cupboards for a large enough container. Eventually he finds a vast china soup tureen ornamented with a rather inept picture of Framleigh; lettering on the other side informs that the tureen was presented to Sir Peter and Lady Standish in 1922 on the occasion of their silver wedding anniversary by tenants of the Framleigh estate. Humming to himself, Greg chucks in the contents of six bottles of plonk followed by half a bottle of brandy and various spices he has found at the back of one of the kitchen shelves. He adds, in a burst of generosity, the remains of his personal bottle of scotch and some gin he has observed earlier in Toby's study. Paula's cooking sherry is a creative afterthought, along with a squeeze from a withered lemon found on the windowsill.

Nick comes in with a handful of green stuff. He is doubtful about some of this, though, and consults Mary Chambers, who discards sprigs of camomile, ground ivy, herb robert and lavender, allowing only the mint and the thyme.

And when at last the late summer dusk arrives there is an agreeable sense of expectation about the place. The french windows of the Common Room are open to the terrace; a cloth has been put on the big table and glasses set out. There are bowls of crisps, and the brimming soup tureen and a back-up supply of bottles over in the corner. Toby brings the old wind-up His Master's Voice gramophone through with a pile of 78s – Cole

Porter and Gershwin and Louis Armstrong. The girls, who have never seen such a thing, are fascinated. Naturally, there is no stereo at Framleigh. Actually, the survival of the HMV is thanks to Greg, who retrieved it last year from a consignment of objects being taken to the new antique hypermarket in Warwick.

People gather. Glasses are filled. Paula is the last to appear. She slowly descends the main staircase, and those facing the door break off whatever they are doing to gaze for a moment. She certainly looks rather magnificent. Her hair is piled up in a vaguely Grecian way, with a good deal of it escaping in twists and coils; she wears a sea-green long dress, also indirectly classical though in fact made in Bombay and still faintly impregnated with sandalwood (that smell, for ever after, will remind one or two people of Framleigh); the cut and texture of the dress make it clear that she has disposed of the problem of how to wear a bra under it by not doing so. She pauses for a moment under the broken pediment of Kent's double doors and looks round. "I could do with a drink," she announces.

The night is still warm. People move out onto the terrace. One of Lemniscaat Farms' stockmen, doing something to a calf in the park, looks across the ha-ha and up the prospect and sees them drifting there in the half-light; they seem some gilded product of the house itself, a manifestation of its style and age and detachment from real life – laughter, the tinkle of glasses, groupings and re-groupings.

"Do you know," says Jean Simpson, "I think this stuff is making me a bit woozy. Mind, I've never had a strong head."

"Writing . . ." says Greg, "being a poet . . . is ultimately self-destructive. If you get what I mean. Art is essentially an act of sacrifice."

"There's someone being sick in the downstairs loo," says Jason.

"Hey!" says Paula, "what's all this? I thought you had a wife and kids stashed away somewhere in south London?"

"I'm not crying," says Tessa, "I've got something in my eye, that's all."

The telephone rings, unheard. The gramophone is playing in the Common Room and anyway most people are out on the terrace, or elsewhere. Bob is showing Sue how to do the rhumba, a dance she is too young to know about. Sue is in fits: she hadn't realized how nice Bob is and wishes she had done more potting. Tessa still has something in her eye. Others are combining in various ways, or wandering around, or simply drinking. Greg has had to replenish the soup tureen. It is having an interesting effect: Jean Simpson is trying the rhumba now, and Sam, who has been so self-effacing, has become noisy and assertive. Toby, feeling maybe that the good name of Framleigh has been salvaged, is genial. He moves around, talking to people. He talks to Mary Chambers. He hopes she feels she has got something from the course and says that she really does have quite a bit of

174

talent, she must carry on with her painting. Course members, when told this, are usually overcome: they bridle and get coy. Mary appears to take it quite calmly: she does not even seem appropriately surprised. Yes, she says, she intends to. There is something about the way she looks and speaks that is faintly disconcerting: she is not, Toby realizes, awed by him or by Framleigh, any longer. Of course, this has happened to people before but it is odd that it should have happened to this rather mousy little woman. Not willing to get further involved, he moves on.

Elsewhere, Paula says "Ow, you're squashing me".

It is dark in the grotto, and scarcely less so outside. The Framleigh woods flutter and rustle. So does the old mattress which is kept there for picnics, Paula explains. Keith had wondered . . . He says "Sorry".

"That's better. O.K. – carry on."

Paula is every bit as marvellous as he expected, and more so. He cannot see her very well, which is a pity. At least only her face, and those breasts. It is what she says that is a bit disconcerting. She is awfully bossy; she keeps instructing. He has always been in favour of the bloke, well, taking the initiative. Paula doesn't seem to share this view. It is all go: this way, that way, on top, underneath. And he is uncomfortably aware of, in the background, a splitting headache induced presumably by that god-awful drink. "You're fantastic . . ." he murmurs, "Paula, I . . . I . . ." I love you, is what he has normally said under these circumstances, but somehow he has a feeling it wouldn't go down all that well. "I think you're the most marvellous person," he ends, lamely.

"What?" says Paula. "Look, shift your leg – no, the other one . . ."

"There's two men," announces Jason, "in posh clothes. With a posh car. And they want Toby. Why's Sam lying on the floor like that?"

"Of course," Lowther explains, "you're missing a lot not seeing it by daylight, but at least you'll get some idea of the ambience." He stands, with Sir Henry Butters, in the hall; he indicates the staircase ". . . Kent's design, of course." Lowther has been doing a bit of homework, and his tone is ever so faintly proprietorial, though deferential also, "Pevsner thinks it particularly fine. This way, sir – I imagine Standish is somewhere about".

"Bit of a party going on, by the sound of it," says Sir Henry. He is not averse to a bit of a party, as it happens, and he has seen through the open door of the Common Room a rather pretty girl standing at the table, winding up some old-fashioned gramophone. Probably just as well Dorothy decided not to come this time. He enters the room. "Hello there!" he says. You don't want to seem stuffy, with people like this.

"I want," says Nick, puce to the hair-line, "to talk."
Toby frowns. "My dear, that sounds so ominous. Talking, in my experience, never does anyone any good." He lays an arm round Nick's shoulder. Beyond the rose-clad wall of the swimming-pool enclosure there are footsteps, a scuffle, a smothered giggle, and then silence. "Just Bob," says Toby,

176

"keeping his hand in. Look, I ought to get back and see everything's O.K. . . ." He kisses Nick. "Why not let it ride, whatever it is that's bothering you? You'll feel differently in the morning."

". . . our Chairman, Sir Henry Butters," says Lowther. "Your girl gave you the message all right? Sorry it was rather short notice but Sir Henry and I had a talk with one or two other members of the Board and it seemed a good idea to have another informal meeting as soon as possible, and since Sir Henry was still in the area . . ."

Toby shakes hands with Sir Henry. He suggests they go through to his study and have a drink.

"Heavens, we don't want to be stand-offish" says Sir Henry. He moves towards the table, and the soup tureen, and Tessa. "Why don't we join the party for a bit?"

". . . and get that fool Sam out of the way" Toby hisses, to Nick. "And get the whisky from my study. And get Paula."

Sir Henry finds the studios awfully interesting. He has a sister, as it happens, who paints a bit. He is very amused by Bob, too, and commissions a couple of pots for the boardroom. In fact, as he tells Toby, and Bob, and Nick, and Greg, they already have a small Hockney in the boardroom, and a Kitaj in the directors' dining-room; Bob will be in good company. Bob chuckles. They have this designer fellow re-jigging all the offices, too, top-notch man, apparently, though Sir Henry admits with a laugh that some of the colour-schemes seem to him a bit far-fetched, but there it is – you get what you pay for. He loves the stables and looks respectfully at the back of Framleigh, from the terrace, and peers into the darkness of the prospect. He has another whisky and chats to Greg: he tells Greg about the differences between being English and being American, tapping him on the knee from time to time to emphasize a point. Greg is simultaneously telling Sir Henry about his current project, so neither hears much of what the other is saying, which is fine. Sir Henry likes meeting all sorts of people; he gets on with people; he is interested in people. This is one of the reasons – as he often tells younger colleagues – he is such a successful banker.

Lowther hovers, thinking about pheasants. Toby hovers too. From time to time he and Lowther exchange a perfunctory remark; neither is certain, any more, if they are in league or at war.

Paula arrives, suddenly, on the terrace. There she is, in the long floaty dress (to the back of which are stuck a few leaves and bits of twig), her hair tumbling from its Grecian arrangement. Sir Henry looks away from Greg. He knows a good-looking woman when he sees one. He rises, holding out a hand. "Ah, Mrs Standish?"

Paula smiles graciously. "Paula," she says, "please . . ."

"Pound-note voices," says Bob. "I love 'em. You can smell the brass. Wonder if old Toby'll pull it off."

"Perhaps," says Keith, whose headache is now compounded with rising aggression, "they're in the market for hand-crafted honeypots as well."

Bob stares at him. Over the beard his eyes twinkle. He laughs, a rich genial laugh. He claps an arm round Keith's shoulder, still laughing. "Well," he says, "well, well . . ."

"What's going on?" demands Jean Simpson. "Why doesn't someone wind up the gramophone?"

Sue is curiously patched about the face: one cheek is pale, the other bright pink – denoting, apparently, high emotion. She says, "Toby likes boys. I saw him with Nick, just now, by the swimming-pool".

"Yes," says Mary Chambers, crisply "some men do. Presumably you knew that."

"Yes," moans Sue, "but not *Toby* . . ."

Mary looks at her. "Why should that upset you so, Sue?"

Sue studies the floor. Eventually she says, "I don't think Toby interacts very nicely with other people. I mean, I don't think it's fair to sort of let someone think you particularly like them, I mean in a particular way, when you don't really. I think that's cheating, sort of. Actually I think it's selfish."

"Yes," says Mary, "it is."

"Actually, I think they all behave a bit selfishly here."

Mary nods.

"Even if they are artists. In some ways they behave even more like other people than other people do. I mean, either you behave exactly as you like, or you don't."

"Doing your own thing . . .?" murmurs Mary.

"Well, yes, I s'pose so . . . But really, that's what children do, isn't it? And people spend all their time telling them not to. Parents. You have to teach them to have manners and be considerate and unselfish. If you just leave them to behave naturally it doesn't do. Actually," says Sue hotly, as the theme gathers strength, "the world wouldn't work if everyone did exactly what they felt like doing."

Paula tells Sir Henry all about her work and about herself and about what she has done and what she intends to do. Paula rather likes older men, though of course Sir Henry isn't really her sort of person at all, but he is an old sweetie and awfully interested in her things. Sir Henry pats her knee from time to time; she makes him think of opera for some reason (that one about the people in an attic in Paris, the girl on the sofa, all that . . .) and portraits in the Royal Academy Summer Exhibition of pretty, flimsily dressed women just called "Celia" or "Clarissa". Women quite unlike one's wife, or sisters, or the wives of one's friends. And the candid stares of girls in French Impressionist paintings and Edwardian postcards of actresses in enormous hats – gay, racy people set aside from real life. "My dear," he says, "you must let me know if there's anything one could do to help. Now this question of extending the studio . . ." Standish, of course, is a bit of a creepy fellow, but still . . .

"I wonder," Lowther says delicately, "if maybe you and I should look over a few figures, er . . . Toby. Sir Henry seems quite happy for the time being."

Toby nods. He looks, thoughtfully, at Paula and Sir Henry; he

180

seems to be interested by the way in which Sir Henry is patting Paula's knee, rather than resentful.

It is night now: deep, still, summer night. The Framleigh woods have almost ceased to creak and rustle. The great mantled black slugs are at work in the herbaceous border and a cat from the village is crunching something by the cascade. The terrace now is empty of people and inside the house it is quieter. Sam, in a distressing condition, has been put to bed by Keith. Jean Simpson is telling someone that her husband sometimes doesn't understand her. Bob and Tessa are nowhere to be seen. Sue has gone to bed. On her way up the stairs she passed Toby and was aware of something very curious: his proximity no longer inflamed the senses – his arm was anyone's arm, his thinning hair was any thinning hair, his faded jeans were any faded jeans. Paula and Sir Henry, at Toby's suggestion, have gone over to Paula's studio to have another look at the soft sculptures; Sir Henry is telling Paula about his little place in Sardinia and Paula is saying she has always loved abroad and she finds she works so much better in hot climates and she gets these foul colds at Framleigh in the winter. Toby and Lowther are talking, intently. Greg is describing to Keith his early poetic struggles and the Creative Writing Fellowship that he is almost certainly about to be offered and Keith who no longer cares enough about anyone or anything even to be maddened by Greg is morosely finishing off what drink is still around.

Nick says to Mary Chambers "I'm not sure that I should go on being at Framleigh." When Mary does not reply he adds, gingerly "What do you think?"

"What would you do if you weren't?"

"I suppose," says Nick, "I'd get down properly to finding a job and somewhere of my own to live."

"Is that what you want to do?"

Nick hesitates. "I think it's what I'd want to do if I hadn't met Toby."

"Then," says Mary, "I think you should probably get on and do it."

Later still, Mary comes across Jason asleep in a heap of Paula's ethnic cushions. She and Nick together carry him up to his room and put him into bed. Mary wipes his face and hands with a damp flannel and Jason, dreaming that a bear is licking him, feebly protests. He rolls over onto his stomach, crossly grunting; they leave him.

The Rover turns out of the Framleigh gates onto the road. The village is respectably asleep, as well it might be. Lowther too could do with his bed, as it happens. Sir Henry, on the other hand, is alert and in full constructive conversational flow. For a man of sixty-three he has remarkable energy; that is one of the reasons he is chairman of an international banking corporation.

". . . Of course Jacobson will have to look carefully into the costing . . . Run as a tax loss . . . Purely a prestige venture . . . Various members of the board will be out of sympathy, but we can talk them round, John, eh? Standish will have to be made to see sense about the asking price. Odd fellow, Standish. A bit seedy, to my mind. Still – he seems very much the guiding light, and the rest of the outfit I rather took to. Mind, one would set certain conditions from the outset. The staffing must remain much as it is. The young chap seemed a bit of a light-weight, I thought, just some art college johnnie, but the others we'd want to hang on to. That American fellow – I like Americans. And the potter – what was he called? Bill, Bob . . . amusing chap. And of course Mrs Standish is essential. Very talented woman, John, very talented indeed . . ."

Toby looks round Paula's door. "May I come in?"

Paula is in bed. She looks over the sheet with suspicion. "I'm going to sleep. I'm shagged out, frankly."

Toby sits on the edge of the bed. "So am I. The courses are so exhausting." He lays a hand on the ridge of bedclothes that is Paula's thigh. "We ought to have more time to ourselves."

Paula stares at him in amazement. She says, warily "Why?"

Toby frowns. "One gets so involved . . . There are so many demands on one . . . The important things in life tend to get, well, pushed aside."

Paula studies him. She does not move her thigh. "What's the matter?"

"Nothing's the matter," says Toby, "I just wanted to see you."

"You'll be saying next," says Paula with suspicion, "that you love me."

Toby, who had not been going to go as far as that, smiles: a warm, confiding smile. He massages, gently, the thigh. "That's silly, Paula. Do I need to? Incidentally, there are one or two things I'd rather like to have a talk about."

"What sort of things?"

"Just," says Toby, "administrative things. Framleigh and so forth. In the morning will do." He moves his hand to the dip between Paula's legs.

"Oh," says Paula. She lies there, not moving. Someone walks past the door. Greg, maybe. Or Nick.

Toby and Paula observe one another for a few moments, in silence. Paula seems about to say something and then doesn't. Toby runs his other hand through his thinning hair, in that characteristic gesture.

Paula, suddenly, pulls back the bedclothes. "Oh, all right, then. Come on."

Chapter Thirteen

In the marvellous Framleigh morning Jason and Kevin are on the terrace. The early mist is again curling up from the prospect and the trees and a shaft of sunlight has isolated the temple so that it rides the landscape like a vision. No one else is about; the windows of the house are curtained still and within people are either numbly sleeping or waking to headaches, shaggy tongues and mental unease.

Jason says "Go on, then". He pees into the lily-pond.

Kevin glances up at the windows, and then down at the pond. "I don't want to," he says.

"I can do it further than you," says Jason. "Much further. Look . . ."

Kevin, stung, unzips his jeans. He looks back again at the windows; down in the village his mother vainly remonstrates. "Mine was furthest," says Jason. Kevin glares.

An aircraft, bound for Iceland, maybe, or Honolulu, or Nevada, lifts from the American airbase and surges across the horizon.

"In aeroplanes," says Jason, "when they want to go, the aeroplane people open two holes in the floor, one for men and one for ladies – if it's raining anyway, otherwise they have to . . ."

Kevin has been to Torremolinos, with his mum and dad. He knows a thing or two about foreign travel. He interrupts, with sudden authority. "They don't. That isn't true, you made that up. You shouldn't say things that aren't true."

Jason ponders. "No," he agrees, eventually, "but it's fun."

"I'm going back to our house," Kevin announces. "You can come too if you like."

Jason shakes his head. He has decided, suddenly, to catch some of the wood-lice that live under the stones on the terrace and put them in the lily-pond and see if wood-lice can swim. Kevin goes. Jason squats, turning stones over.

A thrush blandly sings. Combine harvesters crawl tank-like to and fro across the fields. The fighter from the American airbase has reached the Welsh border. Framleigh sheds a few more flakes of stucco and settles to another day.